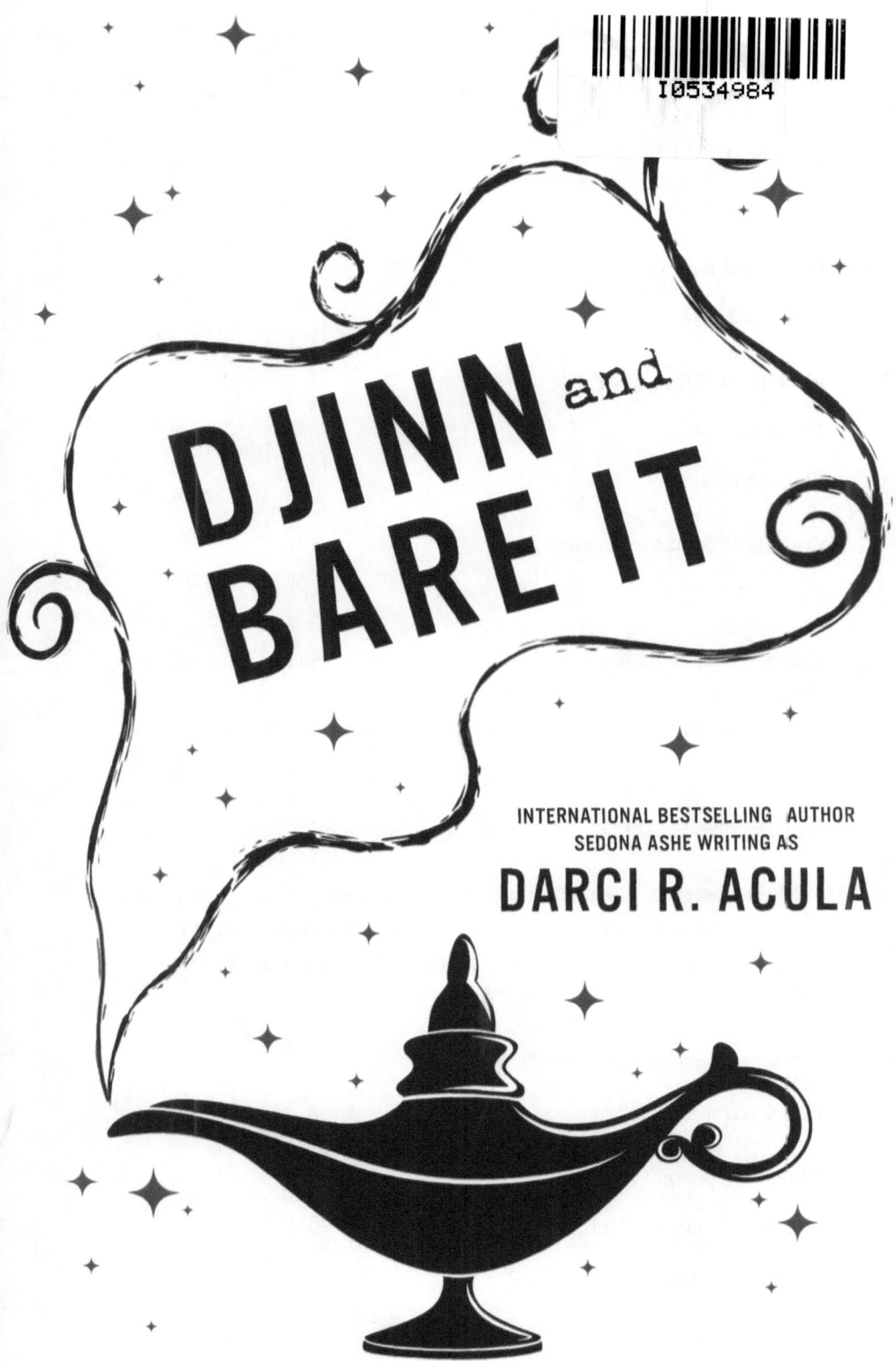

# DJINN and BARE IT

INTERNATIONAL BESTSELLING AUTHOR
SEDONA ASHE WRITING AS

## DARCI R. ACULA

**Djinn and Bare It**

Darci R. Acula

**Must Have Djinn Love**

Darci R. Acula

**Starling Dax**

**Copyright © 2024 by Sedona Ashe**

**Gobble Ink, LLC**

www.sedonaashe.com

Interior artwork by Cauldron Press

www.cauldronpress.ca

A huge thank you to-

Allison Woerner for Alpha Reading.

Maxine Meyer for Copy Editing.

# CONTENTS

# CHAPTER 1

## genevieve

Sinking onto a stack of cardboard boxes on my porch, I took a long drink from my water bottle. When my thirst had been satisfied, I set the bottle on the box next to me and swiped at the strands of hair that had come loose from my ponytail and now stuck to my sweaty face.

I'd seriously underestimated how much work moving was going to be. I didn't care if the island started sinking into the sea and took my house with it; I was never moving again.

Although, I had to admit the view was incredible and worth the work—and I wasn't talking about the almost too perfect lawn or the flowering tree-lined street of the cul-de-sac. My gaze drifted back to the men carrying a heavy dresser out of the moving truck. Their muscles bulged under the thin white shirts that clung to their sweaty chests and left little to the imagination.

*I really should be paying for a show like this...* Oh wait, I already had the day I hired them to pick my things up from Monster Island's shipping dock.

Don't start judging me for being superficial! Until I arrived on the island, I'd only communicated with the movers through email, so I hadn't known or even cared what they looked like. But I wasn't going to claim spending my moving day surrounded by sweaty, sexy, men wasn't an added bonus.

I pretended to tie my shoelace while sneaking another peek at the gorgeous men, especially Charles. He was exactly my type—tall, built like a quarterback, dirty blonde hair that was just long enough to run my fingers through, Romanesque nose, chiseled jawline covered in three-day stubble, and baby blue eyes that could melt the granny panties right off a girl if she wasn't careful.

Yep. He was exactly my type; the type that had landed my poor heart in trouble more times than I wished to remember.

There had been Thomas, who'd used me to cover all the day-to-day expenses while he studied to get his degree, only to dump me the day after his graduation because he wanted to keep his options open as he moved onto the next chapter in his life.

At least Thomas hadn't spent two years stringing me along, like Miles had. After two blissful years, he'd decided he needed to find himself in a cult compound hidden deep in a remote part of the Amazon jungle.

Although, to his credit, Miles had been respectful enough to be completely faithful to me during our time together... unlike Francis. Our relationship had been peachy perfect until I'd decided to surprise him by arriving home from work early.

I'd taken off my dress in the living room and snuck toward our bedroom wearing nothing but skimpy, itchy lingerie. I'd never forget the look of surprise on the naked duo's faces when I opened the door, or worse, the way his eyes lit with hope as he asked, "Threesome?"

The problem was I fell in love too easily, and once I was rocking those rose-tinted glasses, I couldn't see the red flags until it was far too late. My hopelessly romantic heart was so desperate to be in love, but I was tired of picking up the pieces each time it was left broken. As hard as it was, I'd decided it was best for me to stay far, far away from men in order to protect myself.

It was safer this way.

*But also lonely.* I ignored the twinge of heartache at the thought.

It was better to be a little lonely from time to time, than to be sobbing and broken after giving my all to someone who never offered me the same.

"Where would you like us to put this?" Charles' deep voice broke through my depressing thoughts.

The guys were making their way up the porch steps and

I leaped up to hold open the front door that had been closed by the brisk breeze coming off the ocean. "If it's not too much trouble, you can put it in the bedroom on the left side of the hallway."

Charles' blue eyes met mine, and he winked. "Nothing is too much trouble for you, Miss Genevieve."

My heart did a backflip and a set of muscles I hadn't used in well over two years clenched... and I'm not talking about my abs. Although, I haven't really been using them a lot lately, unless you count laughing.

Yep, Charles was definitely going to get me in trouble if I didn't keep a leash on my heart.

Thankfully, before I could accidentally-on-purpose lose my clothes and throw myself at Charles, a Xedef delivery truck rumbled to a stop at the end of my driveway. I expected the driver to hop down and bring the package to the door, but instead, he simply opened the sliding door on the side, and drop kicked the battered box onto the lawn.

Mouth agape, I watched as he quickly put the truck in drive and roared out of the neighborhood. Was this how most packages were delivered on the island? If so, I guess I needed to make sure I only ordered things that could second as a football and had the indestructibility of the plastic batteries came wrapped in.

Shaking my head and making a mental note to call the company and report the driver, I made my way to the sad-looking box. It was covered in red labels that warned the contents were fragile and needed to be handled with care.

*Me too, box. Me too.*

Based on the two dented corners, the odd stain covering one side, and the golf ball size hole in the top, it was a safe bet that no one bothered to read labels anymore.

It was also a safe bet that whatever was inside the box was damaged far beyond repair. Gently turning the package to read the return address, I was surprised to find my mother's name printed there.

Huh. My mother loved buying gifts for people, but she never remembered to mail them. In fact, I couldn't remember ever getting a package in the mail from her.

"Too bad the first one is a bust," I murmured to myself, carrying the box inside.

Oh well, it was the thought that counted, right?

Once inside, I directed the guys to where I wanted them to place several more pieces of furniture, then headed into the kitchen to grab a pair of scissors. Setting the box on the white quartz countertop, I sliced open the cardboard and lifted a palm-sized bronze oil lamp from the deflated bubble wrap.

"Aren't you a pretty little thing?" I tilted the lamp, smiling as it caught the late afternoon sunlight streaming through the window.

Using my sleeve, I wiped the dust from the elegant engravings carved along the sides. I took my time, turning it in my hands and clicking my tongue in disappointment when I discovered a large dent on the opposite side. While I didn't really know what I was looking at and didn't consider myself a collector of antiques, I still hated to see such a beautiful piece of history had been damaged through carelessness.

"Such a pity." I ran my thumb across the dent and gasped as a tiny shock of static electricity zapped me.

"Miss?"

Startled, I spun around and nearly face-planted against Charles' chest. "What?!"

"Whoa! Easy there," he chuckled, reaching out a hand to steady my arm.

My cheeks burned with embarrassment and my temperature spiked, although the latter had nothing to do with feeling stupid and everything to do with the large, calloused palm wrapped around my arm.

"I-Is there something you needed?" I leaned away from him, propping myself up against the counter as I tried to calm my pulse.

The last time it had galloped at this dizzying pace, I'd been failing spectacularly at one of those arcade dance games. My toxic trait was thinking that I could dance, despite having the joints more like those of a wooden tree druid than a bendy ballerina.

Charles' lips curled in a smirk and I wanted to smack myself. Surely he couldn't tell the effect he was having on me, could he? I looked at the ground, offering myself as a willing sacrifice if it would just swallow me real quick.

"I just wanted to let you know we're finished unloading everything. Is there anything else I can help you with?"

*Yeah, I wish you would lift me onto the counter and press*

*between my thighs so I can wrap my legs around your waist while you kiss the breath from my lungs—*

I tightened the leash on my panting heart. This move was a new start, and just because I was stressed about being away from everyone I knew, and slightly depressed at seeing my last unmarried friend post her engagement photos on the book of faces that very morning, wasn't an excuse to fall in love with the next available guy I met.

"No, I think that was all. Your team did such a wonderful job unloading everything. And all without dropping or damaging any of the furniture!" Turning, I pulled three water bottles from the fridge and handed them to Charles. "After seeing how much work moving is, I don't plan to ever do it again. But if I do, you guys will be my first call!"

Charles took the bottles and handed me his card. "Hopefully that means I'll see you around the island then. My personal number is on the back, just in case you ever need a hand around the house or someone to show you around town."

"Oh, thanks," I answered lamely, while fighting an internal battle that involved pulling a burlap sack over my heart and threatening to feed it to the fishes if it didn't chill the fridge out.

Giving me a smile that told me he was well aware of how hot he was, Charles turned and headed out the front door. I watched the moving truck trundle down the street before groaning and gently banging my head on the cupboard door a couple of times. Now that I had a bed and a mattress, maybe I needed to find my sheets and then locate my battery-operated boyfriend to blow off some steam.

I needed to find a new hobby, and quickly, if I was going to stick to my no-man-mandate. Maybe underwater basket weaving? Soap carving? Dirt polishing? Extreme ironing? Or perhaps competitive duck herding? Maybe then I'd learn how to get my ducks in a row... or at least in the same area.

Desperate to do something to distract myself, I picked up the ornate lamp and rubbed hard at the dirt. The lamp coughed and a cloud of sparkling dust filled my kitchen before circling around me like I was the next contestant on a fairy godmother's reality makeover show.

An instant later, the dust took a shape, turning into the hottest blue-skinned man I'd ever laid eyes on, which was saying a lot since I'd experienced a couple of steamy dreams involving blue-skinned aliens after seeing a certain movie franchise.

With his pastel purple eyes, shimmering pale blue skin dusted with turquoise freckles, loose black hair falling around his face, and ripped body, this man was a complete smoke show in every sense of the term.

The gorgeous giant of a man had me on the counter and his broad body spreading my thighs before I could pick my jaw up off the floor. His hands ran down my thighs, gently wrapping my legs around his waist as his lips found mine.

I opened my mouth to— Heck, I don't know if I was going to protest his touch or beg for more, but it didn't matter. Because the instant I parted my lips, the monster in my kitchen used it as his opportunity to deepen the kiss.

My entire adult life, I'd thought I had a talent for picking men who were fantastic kissers, but the way this stranger devoured my mouth made me feel as though I'd never been kissed before. As my mind short-circuited, my body took over, eager to take advantage of the once-in-a-lifetime opportunity.

# CHAPTER 2

## genevieve

If someone had told me that by the end of the day, I'd be living out my wildest kitchen make-out scenario, I would've laughed my butt off. Which was saying a lot since I loved donuts and it showed in my backside.

As his mouth moved with mine, and his fingers dug into my hips to keep me from sliding away, I circled my arms around his neck and tightened my thighs around his waist like I was a koala and he was the last eucalyptus tree on earth.

The only thing that could have made it hotter was if he'd spun around and laid me on the long kitchen island that took up most of the room and doubled as a dining area. We must have been on the same wavelength because no sooner had I thought it, then the guy spun us around and laid me gently down on the island.

He had the height of a basketball player and the bulk of

a football player, but also the agility of a cat, because a heartbeat later he was on top of the counter... never breaking our kiss or releasing his grip on me. The man's hands settled on my waist and his large thumbs brushed my sensitive ribs, causing my skin to flush.

As heat rushed between my thighs, I couldn't help but think how similar this was to what I imagined when I was taking care of my needs. Except if it were a dream, his mouth would be making its way toward my breasts while his hands would be pushing my shirt out of the way.

Maybe I was dreaming, because the man began kissing and sucking his way down my neck, while the heat of his palms seared my skin as they moved up my abdomen.

"Ohhh," I moaned, keeping my eyes closed so I didn't risk breaking the dream of all dreams before we got to the good part.

The scent of bergamot tickled my nose, followed by the cool sea breeze whispering across my bare skin. He shifted his weight to one arm, and his mouth pressed kisses to my collarbone, before slowly trailing lower.

When his tongue swiped across the swell of my breast, I squirmed beneath him, inadvertently grinding my aching entrance against something very hard and very thick. Before my poor sleep-addled brain could process the need exploding in my belly just from that one touch, his hand gently massaged my breast and his tongue flicked my nipple.

"Yes," I groaned, loving the heavy petting and craving more.

His mouth disappeared and his hand moved to the top of my head.

"Good girl," his melodic voice praised as his hand stroked the top of my head. "Such a good girl."

My lust turned to confusion as I blinked up at the man. "Wh-What are you doing?"

His hand paused on the top of my head. "You wanted heavy petting. Isn't this what you meant?"

The man resumed brushing his palm down my hair.

Spluttering, I flattened my palms on his chest and pushed him off me. The mood had been broken, but I couldn't hide a tiny smile. This was the weirdest experience of my life, which was saying something since I'd been born on one of those gondolas that took people between ski slopes and lodges.

This wasn't a dream, and there was definitely a blue man with a magic tongue and hands in my kitchen. I knew when I moved to the island there would be monsters and other paranormals; my boss had included that in my NDA when I signed on with the company.

But I'd been expecting trolls, orcs, werewolves, or vampires. Not a lost member of the blue man band. Spinning on the counter, I hung my legs over the island and rubbed my forehead. Time to think with my head instead of my hormones.

"Sooo," I drawled, trying to figure out how to ask what he was politely. "Are you like a ghost?"

Yes, I'd seen the kids' movie. I knew what the situation

pointed to, but somehow a ghost seemed more believable than a genie.

The man's low chuckle set butterflies fluttering around my stomach. He turned to face me, propping his hip against the counter.

"Djinn, not genie." He reached out and patted my head.

"Stop that." I batted his hand away.

His brows drew together. "But you like heavy petting?"

"Not when you do it like I'm a cat." Although, I might like it if he petted the kitty between my thighs.

The man's eyes widened and focused on my lap. "You keep a feline in your pants?" His fingers brushed between my legs. "Are you sure it can breathe in there?"

My laughter turned to a strangled gasping sound, both from the absurdity of keeping a cat in my pants and his fingers touching me in a zone that still hadn't calmed down from our make-out session.

I caught his wrist, holding his hand still, because I didn't have the willpower to push him away, but I knew I'd be in trouble if he started trying to pet me there.

His blue eyes studied my face, and he sucked his bottom lip into his mouth as he tried to puzzle something out. Finally, the look of concentration faded, and the sexiest little smirk snuck across his face.

"I see. You refer to your genitalia as a cat. Modern language is tricky, but I will learn."

*Focus, Genevieve.*

Releasing his wrist, I took a deep breath. "Okay, djinn. I'm afraid I don't know much about your species."

He shrugged. "That's unimportant. I'm the one who needs to learn about how to best please you."

My heart high-fived my libido at the words every girl wanted to hear.

I reminded myself he didn't mean that kind of pleasing—

"Yes, I do. You own me, feel free to tell me anytime you want coitus or petting. I am happy to provide for all your needs." He crossed his arms over his chest and smiled warmly.

*Back the truck up.*

The blood left my body, my mouth went dry and my lust took a swan-dive down the drain.

"No, no, no." I hopped off the counter and backed away from him. "I refuse to have any part of this."

Blue Dude only lifted an eyebrow. "Which part? The part where you possess me?"

"No! I mean yes! Absolutely no owning and no possessing is going to be happening here." I threw my hands up and started pacing the kitchen as the reality of the situation I was in finally seeped into my exhausted mind.

He shook his head with a small smile playing on his lips. "I can fix many things for you, but not this. You can't unrub the lamp. What's done is done. I'm yours."

"Well, I can't be your first—" I hesitated and tried again. "This can't be the first time someone rubbed you into existence."

I winced, realizing that rubbing one out takes on an entirely different meaning when it's a magical lamp.

The man's features twisted into a mask of consternation. Somewhere in one of the boxes stacked around the kitchen, a clock ticked away the seconds as he stared off into the distance, seemingly lost in thought.

Stepping closer, I gingerly touched my fingers to the back of his hand. "Hey, are you okay?" I whispered.

"I hadn't thought about myself since being awakened. It seems I don't remember my past." His eyes turned to me, an emotion I couldn't place glinting in their violet depths. "I don't even know my name."

From the corner of my eye, I sent the battered Xedef box a glare. Was it any surprise he was a bit scrambled?

"Maybe you just need to rest?" I offered, not having a clue what you were supposed to do when comforting a djinn in a crisis. Offer him a *gin* and tonic?

I could use a stiff drink, but I didn't have a clue where my bottles of alcohol were, let alone my glasses.

"Here." A glass materialized in his hand.

"What is it?" I asked, taking it from his hand and trying not to look suspicious.

How was a girl supposed to know if her drink was drugged so the guy could take advantage of her if he pulled it out of the air?

"I don't need to drug you to get you into bed." He rolled his eyes and some of the tension left his face. "You've imagined us naked together twenty-three times since you've awakened me."

I choked on the ice-cold coconut rum. My mind replayed our interactions, and I came to the belated conclusion that he could read minds. I should have noticed sooner, but it had been a freaking long and exceedingly strange day.

Lifting my chin, I eyed him coolly. "Just because I imagined it doesn't mean it has any chance of happening."

He pushed away from the counter, stepping closer to me. "But it's not just your thoughts." Bending, he took a sip of my drink, then he hooked a finger under my chin and captured my mouth.

His kiss tasted like my favorite rum. Despite my initial impulse to pull away and prove him wrong, I parted my lips, allowing him better access to deepen the kiss. His knee parted my legs, pressing his muscular thigh against the part of my body that kept ignoring our no-man policy.

"Your body tells me you are open, maybe even eager, to have me in your bed," he purred against my puffy lips.

I would've been irritated by his cockiness, but when his hands moved to my hips and rocked me onto his thigh, it was hard to be mad about anything. Heck, it was also hard to remember how to breathe.

He slid me along his silk-covered thigh a second time, and my eyes fluttered closed. "I enjoy how responsive you are to my touch."

It had been far too long since I'd been touched, and what girl wouldn't crumble at the chance to make out with a sexy monster man? For a few seconds, I let myself simply enjoy the moment and the way his every move seemed perfectly designed to please me.

But I was too worked up, and it didn't take long before I

knew we had to stop before I embarrassed myself to the point of no return.

"We have to stop," I gasped.

"I will do whatever you wish." He nipped my bottom lip.

I wished he'd keep going and release the pressure he'd built inside me.

"Then that's what I'll do," he murmured against my mouth.

"Wait! I don't want you to do anything that you don't want to do." With a herculean effort, I leaned my head back and away from the delicious heat of his mouth. A horrible thought entered my mind. "Earlier, when you kissed me the first time…" I paused to catch my shaky breath. "Did you have to because I was thinking about wanting it?"

A devilish smile curved his lips and fiery mischief flickered in his eyes. "I wanted to touch you from the moment you touched my lamp. Knowing your thoughts as we kissed simply gave me the advantage of knowing what you desired so I could act on it. Djinn grant wishes, but we do not have to grant our own—" He must have read the disgust on my face because he paused and then continued. "We do not have to grant the one who holds our lamp the right to touch our bodies. If I didn't want to touch you, I would have stayed in my immaterial smoke form. Now, allow me to grant your wish… and mine." Taking the glass from my hand, he turned so that he leaned against the island.

With a smoothness that stole what was left of my breath,

he grabbed my hips and settled me slightly higher on his thigh so that my tippy toes barely touched the ground. Gripping my hips, he ground me against him.

My body trembled and flushed as he kept me balanced and continued sliding me against him. I stared down at where I straddled his leg. Was there anything more humiliating than being almost thirty but humping a guy like a horny teenager?

"There is nothing to be ashamed of. Stop thinking so much. If this provides you pleasure, just enjoy it." His lips brushed my forehead as he continued the steady rocking motion that was stirring my desire to a boiling point.

I could feel the orgasm preparing to explode inside me and knew I needed to make a decision. Either stop this now or ride the wave.

"Let me give you this." His voice had gone soft, losing all signs of cockiness. "Please."

Unable to think of anything but the lust in my belly that was fighting to be released, I gave in. Circling my arms around his neck, I looked up into his eyes. They'd shifted to a deep purple, and I made a mental note to ask what that meant. Later.

Sensing I was close, his rhythm quickened, and I came apart so fast I would have been humiliated if I wasn't already fully immersed in my humiliation era. Still, I refused to close my eyes or look away as mind-numbing pleasure ripped through me.

The man had given me the best ride of my life.

*On his freaking leg.*

Which totally highlighted the level of lame my exes had been.

"I like this," he murmured.

"Hm?" I panted, still trembling from the aftershocks.

"Earlier you pretended you were dreaming, and I was nothing more than a figment of your imagination." His lips brushed mine. "This time you looked at me. You saw it was me, but you didn't pull away."

I wasn't sure what to say to that. My exes would have just been relieved to know they'd done their duty and eager to stick it in so they could get off. He wasn't making any move to pressure me to take things further.

The djinn slowly lowered me so my feet were on the ground. The dark spot on his silk pants where I'd been sitting had me flushing all over again.

Grabbing me around the waist, he twisted around so that I was sitting on the counter.

He leaned down until we were eye level. "Enough. Your body is sexy, and your pleasure is natural. I like seeing the evidence of your desire. I know little of the men of this time, but I assure you, there is no reason for you to feel upset about having needs and enjoying yourself."

What about what he wanted? What would he expect from me?

Catching my chin between his fingers, he forced me to look at him. "Nothing. I expect nothing from you. And I will accept nothing that you feel obligated to give me."

"But—"

"No." He scooped me into his arms.

I blinked in shock, then slowly took in the room. We weren't in the kitchen anymore. We were in my bedroom.

"You are overwhelmed and your body is going into sleep deprivation. It's time for you to rest." He was so matter-of-fact that I didn't mind his bossiness.

"I can't sleep!" I protested. "The sheets aren't on the bed—"

"Now they are."

"I need to call my mom and my cell phone is in the kitchen—"

"Here you go." He pressed the phone into my palm.

"The guest room needs to be set up for you—"

He shook his head. "I don't sleep. The couch is fine for me to rest on while you sleep."

I was running out of protests.

The man snorted and moved to lay me on the bed. "Finally."

Staring up at him as he straightened and moved toward the bedroom door, I had a moment of panic. I didn't want him to leave me, which was crazy, since I was a grown woman who enjoyed living alone.

"Wait! We need to talk things out—"

He cut me off with a wave of his hand. "Tomorrow. Your body is relaxed. Stop thinking so much and enjoy a good night's sleep."

With that, he vanished, leaving only a thin layer of sparkling glitter on the floor where he'd been.

# CHAPTER 3

## genevieve

Powering on my phone, I tapped my mom's name and waited for the call to connect.

She picked up on the second ring. "Genie! I thought you would be too busy settling in to call and I wouldn't hear from you for a few more days."

"Mom! Did you send me a—" I caught myself just before I'd said *man*, but then hesitated, unsure what word to use instead. "Uh… a gift?" My voice cracked at the end, but if mom noticed, she chose not to comment.

"I did! You got it already?" She didn't bother to mask the glee in her voice. "The island must have a fantastic postal service!"

Thinking of the box being kicked off the delivery truck, I snorted. "Yeah. Not so much. But Mom, what on earth possessed you to send me *this* gift?" I whisper-shrieked into the phone, my eyes darting to the door as though expecting it to burst open at any moment.

"What? A mother can't send her daughter a house-warming gift?" She sounded almost indignant, but I wasn't falling for the fake innocent act.

"Of course you can, but why couldn't you send something like a toaster or a fruit basket?" I paused as it occurred to me she might not know what exactly she'd sent me. It was possible she just meant to send an antique lamp.

She giggled. "Those are so boring, sweetheart! I thought you'd enjoy this more."

*Oh yeah, I definitely enjoyed him —*

Nope. I wasn't going to think about that right now.

"Did you not like the gift? Brenda helped me pick it out, and we were so sure you'd like it."

"Brenda? Are you talking about Bingo Brenda who has the house full of black cats, wears only black clothing, and talks about her family home in Salem that was built in the 1600s? You took housewarming gift advice from her?" I spluttered.

"Well, yes! Don't start up with your silliness again. I've told you over and over she isn't a witch. The black kitties are all failed fosters, and she wears black to hide the cat hair." Mom complained.

Flopping back on the pillow, I put the phone on speaker and laid it on my chest. My head was beginning to ache, and I rubbed at my temples... then thought better of it, since rubbing things had gotten me in enough trouble that day.

"Maybe you should explain to me why you picked the lamp?"

"I was fretting to her about how you were moving to a new city and I just knew you would be too busy to find a man, since you are starting a new job and everything. It seems so lonely, and not very safe to be alone like that in a new place."

"Mom, I'm a grown adult. I am more than capable of finding a guy if I wanted one." My headache worsened, and I wasn't just talking about my mother.

I'd already come to realize that she would never understand that I could be happy without a man in my life—no matter how many times we had this conversation.

"But you won't. You're stubborn," she sighed. "You get that from me. Somehow, you've gotten it into your head that you're happy being independent. But sweetie, I'm your mother and I know the truth."

Swallowing a groan, I tried to get back on topic. "What does this have to do with the lamp?"

"I was getting to that," Mom huffed. "Brenda knew I was worried and told me she had a gift I should send you if I was that concerned."

"Did Brenda tell you what it does—I mean, was?"

"Of course she did. It's a good luck charm that is supposed to make sure the perfect man appears in your life and all your dreams come true. Don't tell me it worked already?" It was her hopeful tone that caused me to blurt out the truth.

"If by *worked*, you mean that the tiny lamp was

supposed to release a djinn with ridiculously beautiful purple eyes, dreamy blue skin, and a grin to die for in my kitchen who introduced himself by kissing me rather than shaking my hand, then yes, Mother. It totally worked!"

For several long seconds, not a sound came from the other side of the call.

The silence was finally broken when she asked, "Was he a good kisser?"

My jaw dropped, and I sat up, staring down at the phone that now lay on my lap. "Seriously, Mom? That's what you want to know? I just told you I made out with a mythical being, and you want to know if he's a good kisser? Most parents would probably want to know if I was taking drugs!"

She had the nerve to chuckle. "Sweetheart, if you found edibles that can create sexy blue men, then you better save a bag for me when I come to visit!"

"Mom!" I yelped.

"What?" She began laughing so hard she was forced to pause to catch her breath before speaking again. "Your father has been gone for years. Even women my age have needs."

I groaned, dropping my head into my hands. Maybe I could go ask djinn-man to erase that mental image from my mind. Forever.

"To answer your question, no. I didn't know the cute little lamp had a man inside. But Brenda has had great success playing matchmaker with a few of my friends' daughters and granddaughters. I thought the lamp was like a lucky rabbit's foot, and we both know you need all the luck you can get to find a good man."

Lying back on the pillow, I stared up at the ceiling. "Why aren't you shocked that I just told you djinn are real? I can't even believe it and I touched him!"

Mom's voice dropped to a whisper. "If I'm being honest, I think you might be right about Brenda. It's possible she could be more than just a human. She's fixed problems within my friend group too many times to count. Frankly, this isn't even the weirdest thing to happen in the past year."

She giggled again. "I think I'll check her brooms next time I visit her. Wouldn't that be a hoot if she has one that can fly?"

If I wasn't utterly exhausted and beyond stressed, I would've been amazed by my mom's open-armed acceptance of the paranormal. I'd already been stressed about having her visit and what she might see, but once again, she proved to be the cool mom. The mom I admired.

That didn't make up for my current dilemma, though. "And what am I supposed to do with him?"

"Enjoy him?" Mom suggested, and I could practically hear her eyebrows wiggling suggestively.

The memory of his hands traveling over my skin caused me to flush. "It's not that simple! I'm too busy with the move and my new job to deal with any added complications. Heck, I don't even know what a djinn eats! Do they eat?"

"It sounds like maybe you should sit down and chat

with him. I know you haven't been on a date in a while, but that's usually how you get to know someone." She offered as though it were the most obvious answer.

"Mom, even if I was in the market for a boyfriend, I don't think djinns go on dates." Unable to continue keeping my heavy eyelids open, I let them drift closed.

"You sound tired, sweetie. Get some sleep and I'm sure things will work out. I love you."

"I'm still annoyed, but I love you too," I grumbled.

"I know you do!" she chirped. "Sweet dreams!"

Tapping the screen to end the call, I placed my phone on the small bedside table. The nightstand sat crooked from being hastily placed there by the movers, reminding me that only one part of the moving process had been completed.

The second half, unboxing and putting things where I wanted them to go, was going to take several more days of focused work. With no small amount of effort and much complaining from my aching muscles, I undressed and pulled the soft throw blanket up to my chin.

My mind replayed the events of the last few hours. The sweet djinn was clearly eager to grant my wishes, but my life was perfect. I liked my new home, my job, and both my mom and myself were in good health. There was nothing I needed or wished for...

But that wasn't completely true.

It had been longer than I cared to admit since I'd been kissed and I'd enjoyed the kitchen make-out more than I was willing to admit, even to myself. The truth was, I missed waking up with my lover's arms wrapped around me while I snuggled into the warmth of his chest.

But I wasn't about to sashay my way down the hall to ask the handsome djinn to make that wish a reality. He already knew far too much about my secret desires.

My fuzzy blanket was the only thing I'd be cuddling that night.

I WAS HAVING the best dream of my life when the morning sun rudely streamed through my curtainless windows and tried its best to awaken me.

Clinging to the dream, I snuggled deeper into my blankets and into my lover's embrace. His lips licked and kissed my neck, while his hand slid from where it rested on my rib cage to cup my butt.

I was really liking where this dream was going, and I vaguely wondered if this was what the podcasts meant when they talked about lucid dreaming. Hooking my leg over my partner's hip, I used it to pull our bodies flush against each other.

What I hadn't been prepared for was the searing heat that sizzled through me like a lightning bolt when his hard erection pressed against me. The tiny triangle of fabric I called underwear created a barrier so thin it was probably see-through. I didn't think my partner was wearing anything at all, but I refused to open my eyes and confirm though, knowing the dream would vanish and I would be left a frustrated mess.

His lips continued to work their way up the column of my neck while his hand gently massaged my butt. Unable to resist, I ground myself against his hard length, gasping at the ripple of pleasure.

It was then that my brain came fully online, showing me a high-speed mental reel of the previous day's unexpected chaos.

"Oh!" My eyes flew open, and I found myself staring at a perfectly sculpted blue chest. There was a beautiful sheen that caught in the sun.

*Hang on...* I stroked my fingers across his chest, then checked to see if any glitter had come off. *Are vampires and djinn related?*

"No, we are not related. I know my memory isn't great, but I don't seem to remember vampires have glittery skin. Is this new?" His voice was husky, but his words still carried the melodic flow that soothed me like a lullaby.

Realizing I was hanging on him and touching him as though I had every right to, I blushed and scooted back. His smile dimmed for a second, but was back so fast I thought maybe I'd imagined the hint of sadness.

Clearing my throat, I asked the obvious, "Why are you in my bed? I thought you didn't need sleep?"

"Because you wished it and I wanted to." His fingers brushed my cheek.

"When did I—" I stopped mid-question, remembering what I'd been thinking about as I fell asleep. "Oh. Yeah."

Maybe I should have been upset that he'd climbed into my bed without asking, but it had been too nice waking up and not being alone. Which was a great reminder of how risky this was becoming if I hoped to protect my heart and mental health from yet another devastating breakup. What if I fell for him and then he finished granting my wishes and disappeared? I had no plans to ask him for anything, but he seemed to take the word wish as literal and I would need to watch myself.

"Let's discuss your questions." He rolled onto his back and tucked his arms behind his head. "My memory is hazy, but I know there isn't a set number of wishes I can grant the keeper of my lamp."

"Keeper of your lamp?" I fought the urge to roll into his side and tangle my leg with his. Why was I so drawn to him?

"I know you dislike the other terms, so I spent the evening coming up with alternatives. This one fits nicely."

Nodding, I agreed. "Yes. I like it much better."

He turned his head to stare directly into my eyes. "But I want to be clear. I have no issues being owned by you. In my past, I feel as though I've held resentment toward others who've awakened me, but I do not feel this way toward you."

It was the sweetest compliment, but that didn't make me like it any more. "I prefer to stick with the keeper of the lamp. At least until I figure out what I can do to undo this."

He studied me for a long moment, then sighed. "As you wish."

33

Wanting to move to safer ground, I asked, "What's your name?"

"I don't remember my name, so I'm going with Roam." His answer was quick, so he must have thought it over while I was asleep.

"It's nice to meet you, Roam. I'm Genevieve." I offered my hand for him to shake, but he caught it and placed a soft kiss on my palm. "But... you can call me Vi," I stammered.

He smirked. "I prefer the name your mother uses."

I sat up and narrowed my eyes at him. "How do you know what my mother calls me?"

His finger gently tapped my forehead. "I'm in your head, remember?"

"That's a silly nickname, and it is even more ridiculous now that I've met you." I looked down, then realized I was practically naked and tried to cover myself with the fuzzy blanket. "Genie and the djinn. It sounds like the title of a rom-com or a fairytale."

"I like the way it sounds," he purred, and an instant later, I was on my back, his body pinning me to the bed. "I understand that I'm an added complication to your already busy life—one you don't need. But until you decide what to do with me and since we are discussing things, I want to make something very clear. You do not need to feel uncomfortable around me or feel ashamed for what you feel."

"I'm not going to treat you like a toy to be used and discarded!" I protested.

*Besides, that would make me no better than my exes*, I added silently.

Roam brushed his fingers down the column of my neck. "Genie, if all you desire is a fling to let off some steam, I'm okay with that. You have been honest with your words and thoughts that you are not looking for a long-term relationship. Stop feeling conflicted that enjoying yourself means you're leading me on."

I opened my mouth, but he continued before I could speak. "If you wish to be petted and cuddled, but then want to go to bed alone, I will not push you for more. If you decide you prefer my body to that of the vibrating worm things in the box downstairs, I'm happy to be invited to your bed. You must understand I'm a being whose life is bound to grant wishes. It is what makes me complete, even if I might have disliked previous wishers."

He paused to kiss the tip of my nose. "Last night, it occurred to me that using my magic to complete my purpose may be what is needed to repair whatever damage was caused during my journey. I know you are content with your life and you're determined not to request anything from me. But maybe letting me grant your secret wishes, those intimate dreams you've been too shy to share, could help both of us."

I stared up into the eyes of the man who was willing to respect my boundaries, give me my space, listen to not only my words but also my thoughts, and let me use his body to make all my wildest dreams come true. It was the perfect offer, so why did it leave me feeling empty?

*Because maybe it's time to consider taking down the walls*

*you're protecting yourself with and give a good man a chance to love you...*

It was a terrifying thought, especially since Roam had made no mention of the L word. He'd offered me the magic wand in his pants, not his heart.

Roam's body trembled and his eyes glowed that deep violet I'd seen the night before, then his mouth found mine in a gentle kiss that was over far too soon.

"Let's get you some coffee," he said, breaking the kiss, and the next instant, my butt was sitting on the cold kitchen counter.

"Good morning, beautiful," Roam purred, pressing a to-go cup of coffee into my hands.

"Thank you," I whispered, taking a sip and moaning as the comforting taste of my favorite coffee hit my tastebuds.

You could only get the coffee from the tiny coffee brewer one block from my previous apartment. It was my one self-indulgent splurge, and I'd been heartbroken knowing I wouldn't be able to get it on the island.

I hadn't wished for it since rubbing him into existence, but Roam had taken enough interest in what I wanted to get me not just a cup of coffee, but to get my favorite coffee. Even though there was nothing in it for him.

Sure, Francis had done stuff like that to seduce women. But Roam knew exactly which buttons to press, or stroke, to make me unable to refuse him. Yet, he wasn't taking advantage of it.

My heart fluttered, and I knew I was in deep trouble.

I needed to figure out what to do with him... because I was falling faster than I'd ever fallen before.

CHAPTER 4

roam

Genie took long sips of her coffee, and I tried to ignore the little moans she made as the warm beverage slid down her throat. It was the same adorable sounds she'd made when I'd explored her skin with my mouth, and had woken her up with soft kisses.

My stomach clenched at the lie I'd told her.

I'd told her most of the truth. The journey had banged up my lamp and my memory, leaving fuzzy bits, missing sections and a killer headache. I'd also been telling her the truth about being fine with her using my body. But that wasn't the full truth.

If I told her the full truth she would have tossed the lamp back in the box and returned to sender. While she slept, I'd grown bored and picked up the book she'd left lying on the table near the couch. It was through that book I discovered what a fling was. No strings, no emotions, just pleasure and fun before going your separate ways.

Genie's thoughts about romance were loud. It had taken more than an hour to understand that she was scared of love, and terrified of giving herself to someone else who would let her down.

Offering her a fling had seemed like my best chance to help her feel more comfortable around me and give her time to see I would never hurt her if she gave me a chance. I hadn't been prepared for how hard it was to offer her intimacy without emotions.

The truth was that it had been love at first sight for me.

I might not have my memories of the individual faces of the previous lamp owners, but I could still feel the resentment and hatred I'd felt when being awakened in the past. Every. Single. Time.

But not with her.

The moment she'd touched the lamp, I'd connected with her mind, something new to me. I'd been sucked from the lamp and into her dazzling presence. It wouldn't have mattered what Genie looked like, I'd already connected with her and I would've thought she was the most beautiful woman on earth.

But nothing could have prepared me for the fiery redheaded beauty with her sultry green eyes, pouty lips, and legs for days. She was built for long nights filled with wild, sweaty sex and had the passion to match her looks, but she kept that part of herself locked away. In some ways she'd been banged up worse than me. I wasn't broken up about losing my memories, and didn't really care about trying to get them back. No, I was spending far more time figuring out what I wanted to do about Genie's.

Her thoughts had shown me what she thought a Djinn was; a kind-hearted, wish-granting, fairy-godfather, side-kick. The only accurate part of that was my wish-granting abilities. But I wasn't bound to just wish granting, and I didn't have to use my powers for good.

Which was great, since I had plans for the men who'd broken her belief in love. I didn't see a reason to scare her by telling her the full truth about what she'd awakened. I was content to be her tame lap dog... until the day she needed a hellhound.

Genie crossed her legs, and the blanket she had wrapped around herself slid off her lap, showing her bare thigh all the way up to her hip. Her hair was tangled around her face, her makeup was smeared, and she was wearing nothing but a ragged blanket, but she looked like a goddess. Yesterday, when she'd awakened me, the primal need to touch her skin and taste her lips had been overpowering, and I'd jumped at the chance to grant her mental wishes.

Having her thoughts as a guide on how she liked to be touched was a blessing, but also a curse because I had to resist going too far. I wanted her body, heart and mind to be on the same page. The last thing I wanted was to make her uncomfortable or cause her to retreat into her protective shell.

Catching my stare, Genie blushed, quickly tucking the

blanket back over her leg. I bit back a sigh, wishing she would feel confident enough to embrace her warm physical nature.

Sex was incredible, but it was more than that. Touch made her feel safe, comforted, and alive. Yet, she kept pulling away, feeling either too scared or too embarrassed to verbalize what she wanted. Her soul was starving, and I could practically feel the anxiety and pent-up stress rolling off her.

If the offer of a fling made her comfortable enough to take what she needed from me to begin healing her heart, then I would be satisfied. And in the end, if she chose to walk away, I'd leave without telling her that she didn't just hold my lamp, she owned my heart.

Genie's stomach rumbled, reminding me she needed food. *I need to go get groceries. Why didn't I at least stop and grab a box of donuts yesterday?*

A constant stream of her rambling thoughts drifted through my mind, it was a welcome change to the hollow ache of loneliness I felt. I focused, sorting through her mind to find her favorite donut. Boston Creme.

I held out a plate with two donuts, "Here you go."

Her eyes widened and she looked at me with the cutest look of awe as though I'd done some amazing thing. "How'd you know?"

"Magic." I teased, sliding my knuckles against her cheek, loving the instinctual way she leaned into my touch.

*Why is he so sweet? Don't cry, don't cry. Oh crap, what if he kisses me? I still have morning breath! I could wish for my teeth to be brushed and then kiss him. No. I'm behaving. But why does he have to be cute and nice?*

*He's a Trojan Horse to my no-man-mandate. Hang on. Do I need to buy condoms for his crotch-rocket? How will I know what size he is? I could pretend to pass out and accidentally grab him. No, that's low, Genie. But how can I be prepared just in case something happens?*

Her cheeks turned as red as her hair and her eyes drifted lower. I waited, hoping she would push past her hesitancy and reach for me.

When she didn't, I answered her unspoken questions. "I don't need a condom. And size can be whatever you want."

Her heart skipped several beats, then thumped out an erratic rhythm.

I pressed my ear to her chest, listening intently and worrying she'd developed a heart problem. "Have you experienced heart issues in the past?"

"No. It's not that." She giggled, sitting her plate down and running her fingers through my hair.

"Then what happened?" I demanded, still straining to hear every quiver and twitch of her heart.

Her hand jerked, and she whispered. "Can't you just read my thoughts and know the answer?"

"I could, but I'd rather you just tell me," I grumbled. "You were thinking about size and I assured you size wasn't an issue because I can be any size or shape you want-"

Her heart did the weird hiccup, stuttering thing again. "See? It did it again!"

I was two seconds away from sending my magic into her, when she squeaked, "Any shape?"

The pieces fell into place and I pulled back, meeting her wide-eyed gaze. "What good is having magic if I can't use it to make your wildest dreams come true?"

CHAPTER 5

genevieve

I wanted to wrap my arms around him and beg him to love me not just in bed, but forever. See? This was exactly what had gotten me into trouble before. I wanted so desperately to be loved and to love someone, I threw out all logic at the first chance.

*This time is different.*

I gave myself a mental shake. That was the lie my heart was telling me just so I'd open myself up, but I couldn't risk it again. It got harder to sweep up the pieces each time.

Taking a shaky breath, I gripped the blanket tighter against my chest like a shield. "I have to go find some clothes and then work on clearing these boxes out of the house. Tomorrow is my first day of work, and I need to get as much done as possible today."

Patting his cheek, I turned and headed up the stairs to my bedroom. It took almost an hour to find my clothes and personal hygiene items. After a shower, and with caffeine coursing through my veins, I felt ready to face the world.

Heading downstairs, I nearly missed the last step when I found the living room completely empty of moving boxes. "Where did they all go?"

Roam stretched out on the couch. "You said you needed to clear them out. I did it for you."

"Okay." I dragged the word out while taking in the bare shelves and walls. "So where are all my things?"

Roam's forehead creased. "What things?"

I put my hands on my hips, fighting my rising panic. "The things packed inside those boxes that I moved over three thousand miles."

He sat up, rubbing the back of his neck. "Oh. I'm sorry. I should've considered that."

"It's fine." I chewed my lip, trying not to think about the memories those boxes held or the fact I would have to go shopping to replace everything.

For some people, shopping was a high-intensity sport, but for me, it ranked right up there with visiting my gynecologist on the enjoyment scale.

"I'll fix this!" he hurried to assure me, and a moment later, the boxes reappeared in the living room.

Soaking wet.

"Oh boy." I sagged down on the bottom step of the stairs.

Roam looked at the boxes, then laughed. "Hang on. I'll fix it!"

The boxes disappeared, then reappeared. Thankfully this time, they were dry and undamaged.

"I guess my magic is still a little wonky." Roam stood, and I tried not to notice the way his silk pants clung to his muscles. "How about you explain what you meant by clearing out, and I can help?"

I couldn't help but smile at his boyish eagerness to help. The dread that had been hanging over me at the enormity of unboxing my entire life slowly eased.

Pulling my hair back into a ponytail, I grinned. "Let's do this."

That happy, content feeling continued to grow throughout the morning and early afternoon. He made me laugh with his ridiculous antics and his curiosity as we unpacked each box was adorable. Roam seemed sincere in his interest in my life, and I found myself talking to him as though he were a longtime best friend and not a man I'd met only the day before.

With his help, I managed to clear out almost all the boxes in a single day. And by the time we stopped to have dinner that he'd *poofed* into existence, I found myself holding his hand as we carried our plates outside onto the small deck.

We stayed outside, talking about nothing as the sun set. Exhaustion from the day seeped in and I had to cover my yawn.

"It's someone's bedtime," Roam chuckled as he stood and scooped me into his arms.

"I can walk!" I protested. "And we can't leave the dishes out here!"

"There. I've taken care of them." He winked at me.

I narrowed my eyes. "Took care of them like you took care of the boxes this morning? Or took care of them as in you put them in the sink?"

"They are clean and in the cabinet with the rest of the dishes." He kissed the tip of my nose. "Promise."

I blinked, and he was laying me down on the bed. "Wait! I need to brush my teeth!"

"Done." He lifted the blankets and motioned for me to get under them.

Licking my teeth, I was shocked to find them minty fresh. This magical crap was going to take some getting used to.

I slid under the blankets and he tucked them around me. Leaning down, he kissed the top of my head. "Sleep well, beautiful."

He was gone before I could respond.

I tossed and turned for almost an hour, feeling restless and anxious for the first time that day.

*Because he's gone.*

Trying to ignore the small ache in my heart, I crawled out of bed and changed into my favorite oversized sleep shirt. For another thirty minutes, I tried to relax and fall asleep, but it was useless.

I didn't have the courage to go find him, but I remembered how he'd heard my wish to wake up being snuggled the night before.

*Roam? If you can hear me, I would like it if you'd come hold me. But only if you want!*

I'd barely finished speaking before his arm looped around my waist, pulling me to him and turning me into the little spoon. Every muscle in my body melted, and my eyelids grew heavy.

"Thank you," I whispered, interlacing my fingers with his and falling almost instantly into a deep sleep.

STEPPING FROM THE TAXI, I stared up at the three-story building that housed Motivated Monster Marketing. Pushing open the glass door, I entered the building and headed toward the elevator. Once inside the polished brass elevator, I pressed the button for the second floor where the graphic design team was located and worked to steady my breathing.

"You've got this." My pep-talk did little to calm my first-day jitters, and when the door slid open, I clutched my portfolio to my chest like a shield.

A large half-moon shaped bright yellow reception desk faced the elevator, and a woman with pink hair grinned at me. She hopped to her feet, causing the dangling earrings on her long, tapered ears to swing wildly.

"You must be Genevieve! I've been so excited for you to arrive! Can I call you Vi? Or how about Vivi? Or do you prefer G?" She practically skipped around the desk, grabbing my hand in a vigorous handshake.

"Um, Vi is fine?" It came out more of a question than a statement.

"Oh good! Well, it's nice to meet you, Vi!" She looped her arm through mine and practically dragged me toward a cluster of desks arranged behind a glass wall. "Team, Vi has arrived!" she announced, then whispered, "the human."

I bit my cheek to keep from laughing. Did she think I couldn't hear her? The woman was still holding my arm as though she was worried I was going to sprint away. Three heads popped up from behind large screens.

"Barker! You aren't supposed to say that in front of her!" A giant of a man with green-hued skin and buzz-cut blonde hair rolled his eyes.

"Why? Do you think she didn't know?" The pink-haired tornado still holding my arm laughed, then turned to me. "I'm Barker, and I'm a fairy. Tiny"—she pointed at the giant —"is an orc."

"Nice to have you join the team. Your work is incredible." Tiny's grin was genuine and my nerves eased.

"The guy with the blue mohawk is a merman and we call him Frost because he's a weirdo who prefers to swim in arctic waters instead of tropical." She shivered dramatically. "Bitzy is a chupacabra, and don't worry, her bark is worse than her bite. Unless you're a goat."

"Stop scaring her, Barker!" Bitzy stood, and I was surprised to see she was over six feet tall. She held out her hand to shake. "Our names don't really fit."

Barker stuck out her tongue. "She doesn't need to be afraid of us. It's Rebecca she needs to look out for."

My stomach pitched. "Rebecca? As in, the owner of the design firm? She seemed so nice on the call…"

"She's great." Tiny's chair creaked ominously as he leaned back and stretched. "But she's going through a rough patch and it makes her a little moody."

"Moody? Try monstrous! Pun intended." Barker clicked her tongue. "But don't worry, they only do this every other month or so."

"Do what?" I asked, glancing around as though Rebecca might leap out at any moment.

"Breaks up with her boyfriend. But they'll get back together in another week or so and Rebecca will be back in a wonderful mood and the best boss ever!" Bitzy waved me toward an empty desk, clearly hoping to distract me. "Here's your desk. Feel free to decorate it and make yourself at home."

I placed my portfolio on the desk and sat down, spinning once in my chair. Despite my nerves, this was the job I'd been working toward for so long. MM Marketing was world-renowned for their top-level design work. They kept their team small, but it worked like a well-oiled machine.

The intensity of the interview process had left me crying into a glass of wine and ready to pull my hair out more than once, but it was all worth it now that I was sitting here.

I barely had a chance to take it all in before the door flew open and Rebecca blew in like a storm off the ocean. Her dark, raven black hair sat on top of her head in a haphazard topknot that looked ready to fall with every step she took. Oversized sunglasses covered most of her face, and she wore a wrinkled dress shirt under a large coat.

"Good morning, team. If you've finished socializing, maybe you'd consider getting some actual work done? We have three deadlines this week, and they should have been done last week." She spoke as she walked, not stopping for a second.

Right before Rebecca's office door closed behind her, she called, "Genevieve? In here. Five minutes."

Silence descended as we all stared at her closed door.

"Wow," I whispered.

"Good luck." Barker squeezed my shoulder, then hurried back to the reception desk.

"It will be fine." Tiny sent me a reassuring smile.

Frost chuckled. "Probably."

"Hush." Bitzy glared at him. "We want to keep her, so don't scare her away!"

I stared at my watch, counting as the minutes slowly ticked by. When it was time to go to her office, I felt as though I were heading to my funeral.

"Have a seat." Rebecca waved toward the chrome and leather chair that looked more like a sculpture than a place to sit.

"Thank you again for the opportunity," I gushed as I sat down.

Rebecca waved her hand. "You don't need to thank me. Your skills got you this job, and the firm is pleased to have you as our newest asset. If there is anything you need to streamline your workflow, please let me know and it will be taken care of."

"That's really generous." Some of my nerves settled at the reminder of why I'd wanted this job so badly. This company wasn't just the best in terms of what they offered to clients, but also in how they treated their employees.

"I'd like you to shadow the other employees this week. Watch how they work together, and how they prepare for client meetings. You are welcome to offer input, but mostly I'd like you to just observe." She rested her elbows on the table. "Once we finish up with these clients, you will start working with the team on our upcoming projects."

"I'm eager to get started." It was the truth.

Many people looked forward to the day they retired, but I loved working. It fulfilled me.

*Plus, it's the only thing I have in my life…*

Shoving aside the depressing thought, I smiled at my new boss. Her lips tightened in what I thought was a smile, but since she hadn't taken off her glasses, I couldn't be sure if it went all the way to her eyes.

"Is there anything else, or should I get to work?" I asked, sitting on the corner of the uncomfortable chair.

"No, I'm glad you're excited to get started. Go ahead." She flipped open her laptop, effectively dismissing me, and I hurriedly left the room, fighting the ridiculous impulse to curtsy or something equally embarrassing.

"She's alive!" Tiny whisper-shouted to the others as I emerged from the office.

"Hold up your arms and let us check for bite marks,"

Bitzy ordered. When I hesitantly lifted them, she laughed. "I'm just messing with you, girlie. Now come on, let me show you what I'm working on."

The hours passed quickly as I rolled my chair between desks, watching my talented coworkers as they finished preparing for an upcoming client presentation. I remained quiet unless they asked my opinion, and by the end of the day, I felt comfortable enough to join in with their banter.

"Alright, monsters—and human—it's time to head out for the day!" Barker clapped her hands and twirled.

"It's a crime for anyone to be that energetic at the end of the day," Bitzy grumbled, saving her files and powering down her computer.

"Agreed," Frost huffed, throwing a backpack on his shoulder. "See you losers tomorrow."

"I'll walk out with you." Tiny rose, his height dwarfing the desks.

Eager to get home and see Roam, I grabbed my portfolio and quickly told the girls bye. At the last minute, I decided to stop in the ladies' room.

I'd just finished using the toilet when the door opened and someone came in. Instead of taking the stall next to me, I heard the rustle of fabric as they headed toward the sink.

My hand froze on the toilet flusher as loud sobs bounced off the copper-plated bathroom walls. I recognized the heartbreaking note in the woman's cries and my chest tightened with immediate anxiety.

Not wanting to intrude on a private moment, but not wanting to make it weirder by lurking in the stall and possibly being caught, I flushed. I took my time leaving the stall, giving her time to escape if she wanted.

But when I opened the door, I found Rebecca still leaning over the sink. She'd taken off her glasses, and was wiping at her eyes with a monogrammed paper towel.

"I didn't realize anyone was still here. My apologies," she murmured.

When she looked up at me, her eyes were red and I knew it wasn't just from this most recent cry, but from hours of crying.

"I swear I'm usually far more put together." She gave a dry, humorless laugh. "But it's hard when I've struggled to eat or sleep the last few days. Frankly, I'm surprised I still have tears to cry."

With that, she placed her glasses back on her face, flipped her hair over her shoulders and walked from the bathroom with her chin held high. She was trying her best to hide her pain, and the memories of having my heart broken and my world flipped upside down came rushing back. It hit me like a punch to the gut. My throat tightened, and I struggled to breathe. I couldn't do that again.

It had been far too hard to pull myself together and show up for work. And it had taken months to find joy after my breakups. I was too sensitive and found it far too easy to blame myself for things not working out... even when my therapist was trying her best to help me see I hadn't betrayed my partners.

I'd worked hard on myself, and I was finally happy again.

Yet, I'd been rushing home, not because I was excited to sip wine and watch the sunset... but because I wanted to see Roam.

Last night, I hadn't been able to sleep until he'd come to hold me. And this morning, I'd pretended to still be asleep so I could enjoy being snuggled.

I was losing my heart to him, and I knew if it didn't work out, I might lose myself again. It was a risk I just couldn't take. Not when I'd worked so hard for this fresh start. I had to do something before it was too late, and I had to do it fast.

# CHAPTER 6

## genevieve

I stuck the tiny lamp in my purse and headed inside the antique shop. This wasn't one of the high-end shops where only the wealthy could afford to touch things. It was a hometown store that was stuffed full of secondhand items to be loved.

I planned to stick the lamp on the shelf and hoped the person who picked it up would be the right one. Like fate or something.

Explaining my plan to Roam had been the hardest thing I'd gone through, but he'd reassured me he understood and had offered to return to the lamp without me asking. I almost wish he would have been angry over it, so I could've felt justified for putting my needs first. Instead, he'd been the gentleman who'd shaken me to my core and made me feel like my feelings mattered.

A spark of anger burned in my chest toward my mother

for putting me in this situation. If this had been a guy wanting to date, I could have turned him down and just went on with my life guilt free and without feeling like I was the bad guy. But I felt responsible for him. Which was absolutely ridiculous since he was likely hundreds, if not thousands, of years old. He didn't need me.

*But you need him.*

Yeah. And that was the problem. I'd smiled more in the past days than I had in years, and it was because of him. What if this was me becoming reliant on another man to be happy?

My fingers brushed along the shelves as I stared unseeing at the items packed tightly in the small space. I knew what I had to do, but I was struggling to find the strength to do it.

Pausing, I slipped my hand in my bag and gripped the lamp. My thumb slid along the surface, and I realized belatedly I was seeking comfort. A warmth spread through my fingers and up my arm.

I pulled the lamp out, clutching it to my chest. Even though I was pushing him away, he was still willing to comfort me.

"Oh, that lamp is lovely!" A sharp-dressed woman in stilettos stepped beside me, nodding at the lamp. "Are you going to buy it? If not, I definitely want it."

"No. It's mine." The words rolled from my lips before I had a chance to even decide what I wanted to say. "I mean, I brought it from home to find items that would look nice being displayed with it."

The woman shook her head sadly. "That's a shame. I collect lamps and it would go perfectly with the others. Let me give you my number in case you decide you ever want to sell it."

I clutched the lamp tighter, feeling a strange possessiveness over it. No, not it. *Him.* I didn't want this woman rubbing any part of this lamp... or Roam.

She dug in her purse and pulled out a gold-etched business card with her name and number. I took it, then placed it and the lamp in my purse.

"If I change my mind, I'll let you know," I mumbled, then rushed out into the dazzling golden hour of sun that came right before it set.

Walking down the sidewalk, I knew I wasn't ready to go home and face Roam's questions, so when I happened on a cute little pub, I headed inside.

I was on my second drink when someone sat down on the barstool next to me.

"If you wanted a drink, you could've called me." Charles' sexy half-smile that had set butterflies off in my stomach on moving day did absolutely nothing.

Maybe because I couldn't get my mind off a certain djinn.

"Oh, hey." I tried to summon a little warmth, but I wasn't in the mood for company and didn't want to encourage him.

"I'll take a beer and give the lady another of whatever she's having." Charles winked at the pixie serving drinks and her wings fluttered in response as pink tinged her cheeks.

Turning back to me, he started a steady stream of small talk. I kept my answers polite but short as I tried to give him the hint that I wanted to be left alone with my thoughts.

Apparently, Charles wasn't used to being ignored, because he reached out to pat my knee. "You seem a little down. Are you having a hard time with the move?"

I stared down at his hand. It was a forward gesture, but not any more flirty than other interactions I'd experienced at bars. Still, it made my stomach flip-flop. There was only one man whose touch I wanted.

"This was my first day at my new job, and I'm just tired." Crossing my legs, I forced him to remove his hand.

Charles sucked air between his teeth. "Whew. That's always tough. Did you enjoy it?"

"Yes, actually. I did." I sipped at my drink and tried to catch the bartender's eye so I could pay my tab and make my escape.

The bar was getting more crowded as people got off from work and piled into the booths. Charles stood, greeting another man who had entered the bar. I breathed a sigh of relief, thinking his attention had been diverted. That relief was short-lived.

"Here man, have my seat." Charles shifted positions to give his friend more room to take his barstool, inadvertently bumping into me.

My bar stool wobbled, and my drink sloshed a bit as I set it down to grab the counter.

"Whoa! I'm sorry!" Charles apologized, wrapping an arm around me. "Here, let me help." Grabbing some napkins, he tried to wipe up the alcohol that had spilled on my lap.

"It's okay. Seriously." I tried to grab the napkins from his hand, but he ignored me.

"Listen, if this needs dry-cleaning, I'll cover the cost." It was weird how sweet and respectful his words seemed, while at the same time his hand was sneaking higher and higher up my thigh.

"Miss?" I called the bartender. "I'm going to leave cash to cover my tab."

Dropping more than enough to cover the bill and a generous tip, I stood. "I'm going to head home. You can have my seat, Charles." I kept my friendly smile in place, but I was honestly horrified I'd even been attracted to a man like this.

He fake pouted, and his arm circled my waist again. "Don't leave so soon. I haven't been able to get you off my mind. Let me buy you dinner."

I shook my head, trying to step free of his muscular body. "It's been a long day. All I want is to go home and collapse into bed."

What he probably thought was a seductive smile slid onto his face. His tongue licked across his bottom lip, and his hand trailed up my ribs. "I've been told I have magic hands, and I'd be happy to massage the tension from your body. After I'm finished with you, I swear you'll sleep like the dead."

*And I wish you'd drop dead...*

THUD.

Charles' body dropped so fast, it reminded me of the little wooden figures that toppled the moment you pushed the button to loosen their strings.

Bar patrons gasped, rushing to check his pulse as I stood frozen, staring at his gray skin and unseeing eyes.

What in the monkey fudging nuts was going on?

"You seriously thought he was hot?"

My neck popped as I twisted to find Roam standing beside me, arms crossed over his chest.

"No! Maybe," I muttered, then a horrible thought crossed my mind. Not wanting anyone to hear me, I hissed, "Did you do this?"

"First, no one can see me except you, which kinda makes you look crazy since you're talking to yourself." Roam jerked his chin toward the people trying to resuscitate Charles. "And second, yes. But don't feel bad. He was going to die tonight, whether you wished it or not."

"What are you, the grim reaper? You can't know when someone is going to die!" I held my hand over my lips, hoping I looked horrified and no one would notice my lips moving behind my fingers.

"I can if I'm the one who's going to kill them," Roam shrugged. "He touched you and pushed for intimacy you didn't want."

"Yeah, that wasn't cool. Guys can be a little pushy when

shooting their shots," I winced. "You should see what happens when they slide into your DMs."

"And I can be violent when I slide into their houses at night." Roam's face twisted in disgust.

"You have to undo this!" I whispered. "I didn't actually want him to die! Please."

Roam rolled his eyes. "Fine. But let's wait one more minute."

"Why?" I asked, suspicious of the mischief I saw glinting in his eyes.

"Wait for it..." The corner of his mouth twitched in amusement at something on the floor, and I reluctantly tore my eyes away to look down at Charles.

Just in time to see a giant orc with a scraggly beard, and half-rotted tusks start mouth to mouth on Charles.

Roam burst out laughing. "Time to wake up, Princess."

Charles' eyes flew open and color flooded his gray skin. Then he saw he was lip locking with an orc and his eyes almost popped out of his head.

"Let's go," I whispered, weaving unnoticed between the gathered crowd.

Roam followed me outside, wiping tears of laughter from his eyes.

"That wasn't very nice," I scolded, although I was biting the inside of my cheek to keep from giggling.

"What? He wanted a kiss. I made sure he got one." Roam tucked a strand of hair behind my ear.

That simple touch had my stress seeping away. His

touch was what I wanted, and I was too mentally exhausted to remind myself why that was a bad idea.

Reaching out, I took his hand, not caring if I looked crazy. "Let's go home."

ROAM WALKED one block before deciding he didn't like walking and whisked us home.

"That's going to take some getting used to." I wobbled as we materialized in my living room.

His arm circled my waist, holding me steady. I gently pushed him back until he sat down on the couch. Straddling his lap, I hooked my arms around his neck and rested my cheek against his bare chest.

"I don't know what to do and I'm scared." It was hard to admit.

"You don't have to make a decision tonight." He rubbed gentle circles on my back. "You're going to make yourself sick if you stay stressed."

"It's hard not to be stressed or feel bad. But it's not fair for me to tell you we're over, and then want to rush into your arms to be comforted. You deserve more." A tear slid down my cheek.

"Genie, you're being far too hard on yourself. You are entitled to your feelings, your fears, your worries, and your hopes. There's no reason for you to feel guilt over them." He wrapped his arms around me, squeezing me tight. "I'm an adult who can take care of myself. You aren't leading me on. I hear your thoughts, and you need to remember I am exactly where I want to be."

He was right. I was carrying the weight of the world and I didn't have to. Maybe I could just take it one day at a time and see where things went. If he was willing to give me a chance to feel things out, maybe I didn't have to make a decision right that moment.

"What if I wanted to kiss you?" My words were so soft that I thought he might not hear me.

"I'd love that." He spoke softly against my ear, his breath teasing across my skin.

It was the note of hopefulness in his voice that gave me the courage to lift myself on my knees and capture his face between my palms. He waited, patient as always, while I traced the lines of his face and stroked my thumb across his kissable mouth.

Leaning in, I brushed my lips across his in a featherlight kiss. His sharp intake of breath told me I wasn't the only one affected by whatever this thing was between us. I took my time, savoring the taste and feel of Roam's lips.

He didn't rush me, or try to take control of the kiss. Tears burned behind my closed eyelids as he let me take what I wanted—what I needed.

"Always," Roam whispered against my lips.

My heart fluttered and heat filled my belly. "Touch me. Please."

"Tell me what you want," he whispered.

"Read my mind," I teased, hoping he didn't notice my blush.

I imagined his hands sliding from where they rested on my hips to cup my butt, and a moment later, Roam's hands did just that. Deepening the kiss, I felt the heat rushing through my body. I craved more of his touch and imagined one of his hands massaging my breast.

Without hesitation, his right hand traveled up my ribs to cup my left breast. I growled in delight and frustration. It felt incredible, but I hated having my blouse and bra in the way.

*Roam, I want to feel your skin against mine. But if only if you —*

Cool air brushed against my bare skin as my shirt and bra disappeared. The feel of his chest brushing my naked skin had me shivering in delight. His hand cupped my heavy breast, massaging and teasing.

Running my fingers down his chest, I hesitated at the band of his silk pants. He'd never asked for my touch; what if he didn't want it?

"I want it." His mouth moved down my neck to my breasts. "You have no idea how much."

My fingers trailed lower, brushing over his hard erection.

"Genie," Roam groaned, his hot breath tickling the sensitive skin of my breast.

When he sucked my nipple into his mouth, I arched into him and my fingers closed around him. We moaned in unison, finding pleasure in every stroke and lick. Desire was building faster and harder as his mouth and fingers worked magic on my breasts. I longed for release, but I needed more.

Too hungry to be embarrassed, I whimpered, "Roam, touch me." Grabbing his hand, I moved it down until his fingers pressed against the soaked fabric between my thighs. "Here."

His finger stroked the fabric twice before he moved it to the side and traced my soaked slit. The intimacy of the touch sent another wave of heat to my aching core and I clung to him while my body trembled.

"Should I stop?" he whispered against my ear, his finger still teasing me.

"You better not," I growled, tightening my grip around his erection.

His deep laugh did crazy things to my insides... so did the two fingers he slipped inside me. Djinn clearly didn't have any issues finding their way around a woman's body, because Roam's fingers found their target insanely fast. I tried to match my strokes to the rhythm he was using to pleasure me.

"Roam!" I gasped, stars beginning to dance in my vision. "This feels too good. I'm not going to last long."

"Good," he growled, his tongue flicking my nipple. "Because I'm not either. Now let me show you what real magic hands can do."

That's when his fingers began to vibrate, instantly plunging me into orgasmic bliss. His fingers pressed on my most sensitive nerves, sending vibrations and warmth straight into my bones, causing me to orgasm a second time.

I continued to stroke his hard length wildly as I bucked and trembled with aftershocks. Roam's hips jerked and his eyes rolled back as he bellowed my name and came apart in my hand.

Exhausted and relaxed, I slumped against him. Roam wrapped his arms around me, cradling me against his chest. I fell asleep to the sound of him singing a hauntingly beautiful song, not caring that I couldn't understand the words. I felt safe and happy.

This was the kind of man I'd wished for all those times I'd cried myself to sleep. But could I be brave enough to let my guard down and allow him past the walls I used to protect myself?

# CHAPTER 7
## genevieve

I woke in my bed, cuddled in Roam's arms. His eyes were closed, so I took the opportunity to admire him.

It was strange that he was the first guy with blue skin I'd ever met, yet somehow it seemed like the most normal thing in the world. Maybe part of me had always known the paranormal existed, because working with an orc, a chupacabra, a merman, and a fairy hadn't fazed me either.

His lashes were so long, I found myself feeling slightly jealous. I leaned closer, loving the way they shifted in color like an oil slick when the light hit them just right. My eyes drifted to his lips, so plump and begging to be kissed.

"Then kiss me."

Surprised, I tried to scramble back, but he caught me and placed a soft peck on my lips.

"You're awake!" I yelped.

His violet eyes opened, and a flirty smile played around the corner of his mouth. "I told you I didn't sleep."

"But you were so still and your eyes were closed."

"Wouldn't it be creepy if I laid here with my eyes open?" he chuckled, and I couldn't help but smile.

"You have a point. That would be terrifying! Plus, I'd be worried about how dumb I looked while I was sleeping, or what if I drooled!"

He rested his palm on my cheek, cradling my face. "You are beautiful when you sleep."

My cheeks heated, and I looked away, unsure of how to respond to the sincerity I could see in his eyes. "So if you weren't sleeping, what were you doing? Thinking?"

He remained quiet for so long that I glanced back up at him. To my complete surprise, his cheeks had turned a purple hue and freckles glittered like tiny stars on his cheeks.

"Are you blushing?" I asked, brushing my fingertips across the freckles. "Why?"

"Because I'm not sure what you will think if I tell you the truth." He looked at the ceiling and sighed. "I missed you while you slept, so I closed my eyes and watched your dreams."

I groaned. "My dreams are so weird! At least the ones I remember are."

My mind raced as I tried to remember my dreams from the night before. Had I dreamed about having sex with him? Worse, what if he saw my recurring dream where I dressed like a duck and did stand-up comedy?

"I can't dream, so it's nice to see what it's like through you."

His words were so sweet, I stopped worrying... until I reached out to hug him and noticed I was wearing pajamas.

Pajamas with tiny yellow ducks holding mics scattered across the purple fabric.

"Roam..." I drew out his name. "What is this?"

A wicked grin spread across his face and he sat up, hauling me onto his lap. "Look! We match!"

The blankets fell around our waist, showing off our matching comedy duck pajamas.

"You saw the dream," I squeaked.

"Yes, and I must say you are ducking hilarious. I especially liked the joke about the hurricane."

"Oh?" I breathed, still trying to process the gorgeous hunk wearing these ridiculous pajamas.

"What did the hurricane say to the coconut tree? Hold on to your nuts, this ain't no ordinary blowjob."

Oh crap. It was worse than I thought.

Roam wasn't finished. "What did the banana say to the vibrator?" Roam grinned. "You're the one shaking? I'm about to get eaten!"

Burying my face in my hands, I groaned, "Could we just forget that dream ever happened?"

"Not a chance." His laughter echoed around the room, and he wrapped me in a tight hug. "You're too cute."

"Yeah, yeah. Whatever," I grumbled, scowling playfully.

Roam stood, lifting me in his arms. "I know something that will mocha you very happy."

"You better stop right now, mister." I squinted at him.

"Stop what?" His eyes widened in feigned innocence. "But do you know why the kangaroo stopped drinking coffee? Because it made him too jumpy."

"That's it! You're grounded!" I realized my pun too late, and Roam laughed the whole way to the kitchen.

"You're lucky you're cute in those pajamas," I grumbled, resting my head on his chest and soaking in the joy he brought into my life.

I SPENT the next four days getting to know my coworkers, and the evenings snuggling on the couch in matching pjs Roam kept creating from thin air. They grew more ridiculous with each day, and I found myself looking forward to seeing what he came up with each morning.

Roam had developed a slight obsession with binge-watching cooking television, and the past two nights I'd come home to find my kitchen looking like a bomb had gone off. He'd been so excited to serve me a meal made with his hands instead of magic. It was so sweet that I barely noticed the burned bits and the overly salty seasoning.

My life was so full and I was almost terrified my bubble of happiness was going to pop any moment. As the taxi turned onto my street, my heart began to race and I wiped my sweaty palms on my pants.

I was going to have to admit to myself soon that Roam was more than a simple fling... and then I would have to work up the courage to ask him if there could be more between us. My mushy feelings turned murderous when the car stopped outside my house and I spotted a woman leaning against the tree in my yard talking to Roam.

She was giggling, and when she turned, letting me see her full face, I realized I recognized her.

The woman from the antique store.

The one who wanted my lamp.

And now she apparently wanted my man.

I was so angry I didn't even bother to correct myself. At that moment, he was mine, and another woman was in my yard and sniffing around him.

But I needn't have worried. Seeing my taxi pull up at the curb, Roam walked away from her, unconcerned that he was leaving her hanging mid-sentence.

"Genie! You're home."

My heart swelled with happiness at his eagerness. It was reassuring knowing he was affected by this thing between us too. I wanted to kiss him. And I wanted this woman, who had no business lurking around my property, to know he wasn't available. Because now I was sure I wanted to see where this could go.

Stepping from the car, I rushed to meet him, throwing my arms around his neck. "Hi, handsome." My voice was breathless, but I didn't care.

Gathering my courage, I pulled his face down to mine

and pressed a quick peck on his lips. Roam's arms circled my waist, keeping me against him.

"Is that all?" he teased. "If you want to make her jealous and mark your territory, you're going to have to put a bit more passion into it. Let me show you."

Roam's fingers slid into my hair, tilting my head to give him better access to my mouth. His lips captured mine in the type of kiss that won awards in Hollywood and could make a girl forget her name. When he finally pulled away, we were both breathing hard.

"Welcome home," he purred, nipping my bottom lip.

"Wow," I whispered, blinking to clear the lust from my eyes and trying to figure out if my leg muscles still worked.

Taking my hand, he led me toward the house. He'd completely distracted me, and I'd forgotten we had an audience. The woman looked like she'd been sucking lemons, but as we neared, she forced a smile to her lips.

"Hello again," I greeted coolly. "Don't tell me you wanted my lamp so badly you've decided to start stalking me." I kept my tone teasing, but she had the good grace to look away briefly.

"Actually, I just moved into a house down the street and happened to see you checking your mail yesterday. I didn't want you to think I was acting like a creep, so I came to introduce myself, and Roam told me you weren't home yet." She straightened her shoulders and strode confidently toward me on tiny stiletto heels.

How on earth did women walk in the grass with heels? I

sank like an elephant hopping through mud on a pogo stick every time I tried.

"I'm Linda." She held out her hand. "It's a pleasure to meet you, new neighbor."

I took her cool hand, refusing to wince when she gripped mine hard enough to grind the bones together. "I'm Genevieve."

Had it been any other neighbor, I would've been excited to meet them. But every cell in my body screamed that I shouldn't trust her. I'd learned to trust my gut when it gave me such a clear warning. Still, I hated being rude.

Roam had no such issues. "Thank you for stopping by to introduce yourself, but dinner is ready and we have plans this evening."

With that, he guided me inside as I mumbled goodbye. Once inside, I pushed Roam backward until he sat on the arm of the chair, bringing our faces almost level.

Threading my fingers through his hair, I kissed him again. Words and admissions were hard for me, so I poured all my emotions into the kiss. I wanted him to feel how much I'd missed him while I'd been at work, and how much I appreciated him recognizing my discomfort outside and putting me first.

When I pulled away, Roam's eyes glowed a beautiful deep purple. "What was that?"

"You showed me how to kiss with passion. I just wanted to practice to make sure I didn't forget." Not wanting to lose my nerve, I blurted out what I'd been anxious to ask him.

"It's the Rose Festival in town this weekend, and my coworkers are going and I thought it would be a fun way to get to know people. So I wanted to ask if you would go with me." I swallowed hard and twisted my fingers. "As my date. But if you're busy, or just don't want to, I totally understa—"

"I'd be honored." Roam caught my hands in his, stopping me from dislocating something with how hard I was wringing them.

"Thank you!" Relief and excitement surged through me and I threw myself at him, sending him toppling back onto the couch.

Landing on top of him, I covered his face in quick, exuberant kisses. It didn't take long for those kisses to grow longer and more heated. There was no denying I wanted this man, but I was afraid if I opened the dam holding back the love I'd stored up, I might drown him in it.

I reluctantly stood, knowing I needed a few minutes to collect myself before my idiotic heart started declaring our undying love.

Roam's glowing eyes watched me head up the stairs, and a small smile curved his lips.

It was so nice to be home. And I was beginning to realize it wouldn't be home without him.

# CHAPTER 8

### genevieve

"A re you sure about this?" Roam asked as we walked down the street toward the center of town. "I'm sure your coworkers are going to have questions if they see us together."

"Absolutely positive." Interlacing my fingers through his, I smiled shyly up at him. "Are you okay if they assume you're my boyfriend?"

"Are you?" His playful expression turned serious.

"Yes." My cheeks burned, and I stared hard at the sidewalk as though stepping on the next crack truly might break my mama's back.

His fingers curled tighter around mine, sending warmth tingling up my arm. "Then I'm happy to be your fake boyfriend."

My heart thudded wildly, and I stopped walking,

pulling him to an abrupt stop. "How would you feel about being my real boyfriend?"

Roam used my hand to pull me against his chest. "I'd like that very much."

"You aren't agreeing just because I am the keeper of your lamp, right?" I voiced the concern that still lingered in my mind.

He shook his head in amusement. "Genie, you've yet to voice a single wish out loud. Nothing I have done is because I was forced. Bits and pieces of my memory continue to return, and I can assure you this is the first time I've had complete freedom to do whatever I wanted."

I sucked my bottom lip into my mouth. "What if you only like me because of that?"

His laugh was beautiful, and I felt myself swooning. "My innocent little human. I'm a djinn. We do the minimum required to satisfy the curse that binds us to grant wishes. If I didn't have feelings for you, we wouldn't even be talking. I think about you every hour of the day and night because I want to and I can't help myself."

Wrapping my arms around his jean-clad waist, I pressed my face to his black tee and enjoyed the comfort that touching him brought me. "I'm scared."

"I know. It's okay." He kissed the top of my head. "We can go as fast or as slow as you want. There is no rush."

I cleared my throat. "I know you offered me the use of your body for a fling, but if we are trying out a serious relationship, then I'd like it to be mutual. I'm not sure when I'll be ready for sex, but aside from that, I want us to feel comfortable touching each other whenever and wherever. You act on my thoughts, but I'd like my boyfriend to know it's okay to act on his own thoughts too."

He said nothing, but his fingers dug into my hips. My body flushed, and I worried he thought I was being too forward.

"Are you sure? I have a lot of thoughts." His husky voice sent slick heat rushing between my thighs.

"Is that a promise or a threat?" I asked, half-tempted to turn and drag him back to the house.

His hands moved to cup my butt, and he lifted me, then twisted around to pin me against the tall white fence that ran along the sidewalk. I gasped and wrapped my legs around his waist.

Roam ground his pelvis against me, letting me feel the exact breadth and length of his desire. "I'll ask again, my sweet Genie. Are you sure? You have no idea how much I'm holding back, or how often I force myself not to touch you because I don't want to overwhelm you."

I was still terrified that I would end up heartbroken and a broken shell of myself. But I knew without a doubt he was worth the risk.

"You might be surprised." I brushed my lips against his. "It might be you who is overwhelmed."

"I wish you'd try," he teased. "Now, we better get to the festival or we might not make it at all."

Disappointment flared in my chest, but he was right. Besides, we had all night to explore each other's bodies.

Fifteen minutes later, we were sitting at picnic tables,

sipping lemonade and eating funnel cake with my coworkers. They'd accepted Roam without even a raised eyebrow, although Bitzy had winked at me to show her approval, and Barker had pretended to fan herself after shaking his hand.

Yeah, my boyfriend was hot.

Roam never stopped touching me. If we weren't holding hands, then he had a hand on my lower back, or his palm resting on my thigh.

It wasn't possessive or sexual; it was as though he wanted the reassurance I was close. It made me wonder how often he'd been around crowds, if ever.

When we finished eating, our small group moved through the festival, enjoying the booths overflowing with fresh roses of every imaginable color. Every booth had something unique to admire, and I spent far too much time leafing through edible flower cookbooks, admiring kitchen knives with rose petals arranged in their clear resin handles, and stunning rose-themed paintings by local artists.

Two separate times I thought I could feel someone staring at me, and would turn to catch sight of a dark-haired woman melding into the crowd. I tried to calm the flash of panic by reminding myself she lived on the island and I was bound to run into her—especially at community events. Just because she was attending the rose festival too didn't mean she was out to get me.

"Are you okay?" Barker whispered, tucking her arm through mine. "You keep looking over your shoulder."

"I'm fine. Probably just overthinking things." I forced a laugh and tried to relax my tense muscles.

"I know just the thing to get you out of your head!" Barker's eyes sparkled and her ears twitched in excitement. "Let's put you in the dunking booth!"

"I don't know—"

"It's for charity! How can you say no to helping a good cause?" She blinked up at me with what I guessed was the fairy version of begging puppy eyes.

"But I don't have a bathing suit!" I protested.

Roam tapped my tote and winked. "Yes, you do. I packed one."

"Yay!" Barker squealed. "Bitzy! Go tell the announcer we have a dunking booth victim—I mean, volunteer. I'm going to take Vi to get changed! Let's go!"

There was nothing I could do but laugh as she dragged me to get changed... right up until I saw the size of the bikini the naughty djinn had conjured up for me.

I was going to kill him.

"STOP HIDING! If I had legs like those, I'd be showing them off at every opportunity!" Barker grabbed my arm and pulled me toward the dunking booth. She was shockingly strong for someone so tiny. "Seriously, you look fab! Guys are going to be lining up to have a chance to get you wet!"

"Maybe this isn't a good idea," I muttered, feeling self-conscious.

While the bikini covered all the important bits, and wasn't scandalous, I wasn't used to showing off so much skin. It was something I probably needed to get used to since bathing suits were everyday wear here on the island.

Despite my protests, a few minutes later, I found myself sitting inside the dunking booth. The announcer reminded everyone this was for charity, and a line formed, ready to send me plunging into the water.

I searched the crowd but couldn't find my tall, blue hunk anywhere. Maybe he'd gone to the restroom. Did djinn go to the bathroom?

An older guy stepped to the pitching line and tossed his three balls at the target. They all missed, and he stepped out of the way to let the next person take his place.

That's when I heard Roam whisper behind me. "I'm not visible right now, so don't turn around."

Pretending to wipe water from my face, I mumbled, "What are you doing in here?"

"You did say I could touch you whenever." His hands slid down the bare skin of my back, pausing to tease the thin tie holding my top in place.

"I did," I breathed, hoping the woman tossing balls at me would hit the target... but also hoping she wouldn't.

"You also said wherever." His fingers brushed along my stomach. "I want to touch you, and no one is able to see what is happening unless your face gives it away."

I pretended to cover my face in mock panic as the

woman tossed a second ball and whispered, "What are you talking about?"

He pressed a kiss to the top of my foot, then began kissing his way up my calf and thigh.

My legs trembled, and the announcer roared with laughter. "Miss Vi is up here shaking, folks! How about someone who can actually step up and put this little lady out of her misery?"

Roam clicked his tongue. "You're going to have to do better than that."

Clenching my teeth, I braced myself for where he might touch me next. Unable to see him, I had to rely solely on touch to know where he was at.

His tongue trailed up my stomach, and I fought my shiver. *This isn't fair*, I thought toward him, pretty sure he could hear me.

"Maybe not. But it's fun," he growled, nipping my neck while his fingers ran over my skin.

His fingers, lips and tongue continued to touch, stroke and tease until my body was on fire and I was pretty sure steam was going to rise from the water if I ever got dunked.

"I'm keeping them from hitting it." His devilish chuckle had my heart-rate spiking.

Or maybe it was the way he was placed kisses down my spine, from my neck to the band of my bikini bottoms that was causing blood to pound in my ears.

*There's a lock on the changing room door. If you let them dunk me, we could—*

I didn't get to finish before my seat dropped and I plunged beneath the water.

*That wasn't nice!* I thought as loudly as possible, hoping the volume would carry.

His sexy laughter brushed my mind. *I'll make up for it as soon as you get to the changing room.*

# CHAPTER 9

## genevieve

Twisting the lock on the changing room door, I leaned my back against it and searched the room. There was no sign of my boyfriend.

"Roam?" I whispered.

When he didn't answer, I pushed away from the door and walked toward the wooden bench seat against the wall.

"There's something I don't understand." His arms circled my waist from behind, and he pressed a soft kiss on my shoulder.

I covered his hands with mine and twisted my head to the side to smile at him. "Let's hear it."

"While I waited for you to arrive, Charles walked by with another guy. He was whining about how you kept causing him to have blue balls." Before I could figure out how to feel about that, Roam continued. "I have blue balls all the time. What is he complaining about?"

I couldn't help it; I burst into laughter. Spinning around in his arms, I kissed him between giggles. He gave me a confused look, but returned my kisses.

"Are you sure I can't kill him again? I don't like that man," Roam grumbled playfully.

"No killing." I wiggled a warning finger at him.

Roam sighed. "Fine. I'll restrain myself. But if he touches you again, I make no promises."

Wanting to change the subject, I leaned into him. "Now, how are you going to make up for torturing me in the dunking booth?"

"Let me show you." A wicked smirk curved his lips, and he backed me up until my legs bumped the bench.

His fingers untied the strings on my bikini top, letting the wet fabric fall to the floor. My nipples hardened, and a chill ran across my skin as the water trickling down my skin cooled.

"Let me help with that." He leaned forward, his warm breath swirling over my skin in a way that had to be magic.

My skin wasn't the only thing that heated as the water droplets disappeared. "That feels incredible. Could you do this for me after every shower?"

It was meant to be a joke, but Roam responded without hesitation. "Absolutely. It would be my pleasure."

Roam's hand moved to cup one of my breasts, eliciting a groan from me. "How are you so beautiful? Do you know how many women wish for a beauty like yours? Not even djinn magic could make that happen."

"You sure know how to flatter a girl." I ran my fingers through his hair.

He was so incredible, and I couldn't help but wonder how many women had experienced this type of intimacy with him.

"It isn't flattery, it's the truth." Dipping his head, he sucked my nipple into his mouth.

I didn't want him to know how badly I wanted that to be true. "Maybe you just don't remember? You were shaken up pretty bad."

"I remember more each day, and in all my years of life, there hasn't been a woman I wanted. I hadn't experienced sexual desire until you touched my lamp." He spoke between kisses, his mouth giving equal attention to each breast.

My stomach fluttered.

"Now let's get these out of the way." He ran his fingers down my ribs to my hips, stopping when they found the ties holding up my bottoms.

My heart pounded and my breath caught in my throat. What was he planning?

Roam paused, giving me time to protest or push his hands away. When that didn't happen, he dropped to his knees. Using his teeth, the crazy, sexy djinn undid first one tie and then the other.

My bikini fell to the floor, leaving me bare and trembling in front of him. I stood motionless, waiting to see what he would do. His fingers brushed up the outside of my thighs with an almost reverence.

Leaning forward, he placed a soft kiss between my thighs, directly above my slit. I struggled to draw in a breath, and a desperate need unfurled in my stomach.

He gently pushed me down on the bench. When I tried to scoot back, he stopped me, keeping my butt right on the edge of the bench.

"Open your legs, my love," he whispered, voice husky.

I knew it was just a nickname, but hearing him saying the L word had my lovesick heart do cartwheels. Feeling shy, I hesitated. It was one thing to let him touch me and move me how he wanted, but displaying myself to him was a completely different level of intimacy. What if he found me unattractive?

"Impossible," Roam snorted. "Genie, I didn't mean to make you uncomfortable with my request." He paused, then admitted softly, "I liked the idea of you opening yourself to me."

My heart melted at the flash of insecurity in his eyes. All this time, I'd enjoyed the fact that he could read my thoughts and act on them. I was still struggling with verbalizing what I wanted, but maybe it was time I worked on showing him how I felt.

Swallowing the lump in my throat and with my face feeling as though it were on fire, I slid my legs apart. Difficult as it was, I met his eyes and didn't look away as I offered myself to him.

Roam's eyes glittered and began to glow. I'd never seen a man who looked even half as good as the man kneeling in front of me.

"You're so gorgeous," I whispered, reaching trembling fingers out to stroke his jaw. "And you're mine." Realizing how that sounded, I hurried to correct myself. "Not because of the lamp keeper thing, but because of the boyfriend thing."

Except I knew I wanted more than a boyfriend and girl-friend relationship. I was terrified, but I wanted him to be mine for as long as he would put up with me.

"Yes, I am yours." Roam brushed the back of his finger down my slit.

The touch was featherlight, but it nearly caused my eyes to roll back in my skull. Hooking my legs over his shoulders, Roam's deep purple eyes met mine, then drifted over my breasts, down my stomach, and finally between my thighs.

My body trembled as Roam began placing erotic kisses from my knee up the inside of my thigh. He continued moving ever closer to the part of me that begged for his attention.

"Roam?" My voice wobbled.

"Hm?" he hummed, his tongue tracing intricate swirls on my legs.

"I've never been, uh, well, kissed, um… there." It was hard to admit, and I thought he might have already gathered that little tidbit from my mind.

However, the widening of his eyes and the tightening of his fingers on my thighs told me he hadn't. "No one has tasted you?"

I shook my head, and an expression that could only be described as hunger settled on his face.

"You belong to me." The feral possessiveness in those four words had my fears and worries melting away, leaving nothing but the overwhelming desire to be his.

"Yes," I agreed.

"Genevieve, I don't just want your body. I will wait forever if needed, but I want your heart to belong to me." I'm not sure how I would have responded, because he pressed the heat of his mouth against my entrance, stealing away my ability to speak.

My back arched, and Roam's hands gripped my waist and back. He continued to support my quivering body as his tongue traced along my slit. When his tongue delved inside the first time, I screamed his name and squirmed against the intensity of the sensations he'd stirred.

Roam growled, and something in the air shifted. His hands slid from my waist to cup my butt, lifting it off the bench. Gone were the soft kisses and gentle teasing. His tongue plunged inside me, rough and demanding.

As I murmured nonsensical noises, he continued lapping and sucking as though he were starving. The dark lust in my belly swirled and grew with each stroke of his tongue.

"I didn't know it would feel like this!" I gasped.

Sure, I'd been a little annoyed that my exes had been willing to receive but not give when it came to oral. But if I'd known it was like this, I would have been more vocal about my needs.

"No one else is going to taste you." Roam looked up for a moment, and I stared in shock at his eyes. They'd turned such a dark shade of purple they almost looked solid black. "And no one can please you the way I can."

His mouth dropped back between my legs, and this time when his tongue pushed inside me, it was different. It stretched me, plunging deeper than it had before and flicking an erogenous spot I didn't even know I possessed.

He all but sucked the orgasm from my body. My legs tightened over his shoulders as I screamed his name and stars sparkled in my vision. Roam didn't let up and continued to stroke me as I rode the aftershocks.

The dang djinn didn't give me a chance to recover before turning his tongue as cool as ice. It should have been an instant mood killer, but the contrast of the heat and cold caused fireworks to explode inside me. I came apart a second time, and with a violence that left me struggling not to pass out.

"What... are you doing... to me?" I moaned.

"Your arousal is sweet on my tongue and I refuse to share it or your beautiful body. I am making sure no other male will ever be able to satisfy you," Roam snarled, his eyes still dark with the fierce possessiveness etched on his face.

He wasn't lying. I knew without a doubt oral by anyone else could never compare. And if we ever had sex, I knew sex would be ruined completely for me too.

"I'm going to crave this every day," Roam rumbled, placing tender kisses along my inner thighs.

He wouldn't get any complaints from me, and I made a mental note to check into permanent ways to keep the bush cleared away and the landscape smooth. That was assuming I ever found the energy to leave the small changing room. Because I was having serious doubts about whether I still had the ability to walk. How was I going to get home? All I wanted was to curl up and go to sleep... in Roam's arms.

I blinked to clear my vision, and when I opened my eyes, I was staring up at my bedroom ceiling.

"I've shifted your coworkers' memories. They will remember you talking to them and then saying you need to get home," Roam answered my worries before I even had time to organize my thoughts.

He lay down beside me and I immediately scooted into his arms, throwing a leg over his hips and clinging to him like an octopus. If he hated it, too bad. He'd broken down my walls, and I had a lot of love to give.

"I wouldn't mind if you clung to me like an octopus all the time," Roam chuckled. "Now sleep, because I'm not sure how long I can wait before I need to taste you again. I'm afraid I might be addicted."

Satisfied as I was, my muscles spasmed and heat flickered in my belly.

How did I get so lucky?

CHAPTER 10

roam

Genie's breathing changed, alerting me to the fact she was awake. Remembering how much she'd enjoyed being able to study me when my eyes were closed, I remained motionless and waited to see what she'd do.

To my surprise, she pushed the blankets back and left the bed. I listened to the sounds of running water as she brushed her teeth and had to bite my lip to keep from laughing. Stubborn little woman still refused to wish for anything.

Turning off the water, she returned to the bed. Instead of taking her spot beside me, she gently straddled my chest. My heart pounded as I felt her bare, silky heat warming my skin.

"Roam?" Her sweet morning voice held a husky note

that had me wanting to do all sorts of naughty things to her.

She'd opened her heart to me and given me a chance to win her love. And I was finding it insanely difficult to keep my hands and mouth off her.

Cracking open one eye, I gave her a half smile. "Yes, my sweet?"

Her thoughts were a wild jumble, and I struggled to sort them.

"I want to touch you." Her cheeks turned pink, but she refused to look away.

"You are touching me," I pointed out, reaching up to pinch her adorable butt gently. Realizing she wanted permission before she explored, I added, "But yes. You can touch me whenever and wherever."

She grinned mischievously and slid down my body. It took my brain several seconds to finish sorting her thoughts, and by the time I did, she was already freeing my erection from my pants.

"Genie—" I breathed as her mouth closed around the tip.

My size was a challenge, and wanting her to be comfortable, I adjusted my size to fit easier.

She immediately released me from her mouth and growled, "What the heck, Roam?"

"I didn't want to hurt you, so I adjusted my size for you." Despite how badly I wanted to beg her to go back to licking, I nearly laughed at her disgruntled scowl. You'd think I'd taken away her favorite toy or dessert.

"But this isn't your natural form, is it?"

"No, but that doesn't matter—"

"It matters to me. I want to experience this with your true self. You've given me so much pleasure, and I want to give you—the real you—the same."

How did I get so lucky? I was an expert on wishes, but never in billions of years could I have figured out how to wish for someone as perfect as her to come into my life.

"Besides, I love challenges, and my mom didn't raise a quitter!" She slid a single finger down my adjusted length and shot me a sly grin when it caused me to tremble. "I'll get started again as soon as you go back to your natural size."

I controlled some of the wildest magic on this earth, but she held all the power... and she knew it.

This woman was going to be trouble, and I couldn't love her more. Unable to resist her teasing and desperate to feel her mouth on me again, I gave in.

The moment the shift finished, Genie eagerly slid her hand up my length, then without hesitation, took me deep into her mouth. I groaned in bliss as she swallowed, using her throat to squeeze my cock.

Her tongue swirled and stroked my hypersensitive skin, driving me insane and pushing my arousal to new heights.

Genie's moan of delight told me she'd tasted the first drop of my arousal.

Her hungry eyes locked on my face, and she released me from her mouth to ask, "What is that?"

I pushed myself on my elbows to look at her. "Djinn

don't taste like humans, or so I've been told. Our bodies are supposed to provide our partners pleasure during all acts of intimacy, and tasting like a dessert is part of that."

Her tongue swirled over the head of my cock, causing us both to moan in pleasure.

"I can't do the magical things you did to me, but I wish I could ruin sex for you too. Then you'd never want anyone else," she admitted, licking and teasing me until I was struggling to concentrate.

"I've never linked with someone while still inside my lamp. You're the first person whose thoughts I've been able to hear." Reaching down, I sank the fingers of my right hand into her thick hair and forced her to look me in the eye. "Everything about you is magic. You are the only woman for me."

Emotions whirled in her mind like a tornado, moving so fast I couldn't pick out the individual thoughts. Although maybe that had something to do with the way she turned her full attention to tasting me. Pleasing me.

I thought it would have been impossible to grow harder or more aroused, but staring at her mouth around my cock had me swelling to a painful level. She had stroked me to release with her hands, but being enveloped in the heat of her mouth was on an entirely different level.

My fingers were still in her hair, and needing to express my love through touch, I began to massage her scalp. Genie moaned, and I hissed as the sound sent vibrations rippling through my length.

Blood pounded in my ears and my breathing grew harsh. The need to release the lust created by touching her and being touched by her built to dangerous levels inside me.

"Genie." Gripping her hair, I pulled her mouth free, not wanting to surprise her by exploding in her mouth or creating a mess all over her. "I'm going to come."

She gave me a look as though I were the stupidest person on earth. "That's kinda the point."

I laughed, the sound harsh and slightly desperate. Using my free hand, I gripped my aching cock, angling it away from her. "I need to take care of this, then I will return to cuddle."

Genie's growl was shocking and completely adorable. "What the heck, Roam? I'm the one who just learned how to swallow a freaking sword!" Pushing my hand away, she licked the shiny bead off the tip. "I earned this. Now lie down and let me love you."

She was so intent on winning she didn't realize her word slip. I listened to her thoughts spin in circles every day as she tried to come to terms with how she felt. This was different, and every muscle in my body went taut as a glow like nothing I'd ever felt warmed the emptiness that had been inside me for as long as I had existed.

*Let me love you.*

I'd never forget those four words for as long as I lived. She didn't just tell me she loved me, she wanted to show me with her actions.

Djinn granted the wishes of others, serving one owner after another. No one cared to ask what a djinn might want or need.

*Let me love you.*

Tears blurred my vision, shocking me since I hadn't even known djinn could cry. Blinking furiously, I tried to clear my vision, wanting to watch my Genevieve.

This sex goddess driving me wild with her mouth and tongue was mine. Nothing had ever belonged to me other than my lamp, but even that wasn't truly mine. Until now.

She'd given me her heart. And I would spend every day making sure she never had second thoughts about me.

It was all too much, and I roared her name. I'd thought the release she'd given me with her hand had been incredible, but it was nothing compared to this. My need, lust, and emotions had shaken me much like a champagne bottle.

I tried to push her away gently, not wanting to choke her, but the stubborn little human remained stuck to me like an octopus. It seemed she hadn't been joking about that. I couldn't control my groans of pleasure as her mouth milked every last drop of candy-sweetness from me.

She made the cutest little noises of muffled delight as she switched to licking me like a lollipop, delighting in the way my body jerked and trembled at her touch. I made a mental note for future dates to remember how much the little minx enjoyed feeling in control.

"Genie, are you okay? I thought you might be sleeping, but then I heard you moaning—"

An older version of Genie appeared in the open doorway.

My jaw dropped. How had anyone gotten into the house without me knowing? Oh yes, I'd been mesmerized by the love of my life.

"Mom?" Genie squeaked, and I winced when her fingers tightened around my erection.

# CHAPTER V

## Genevieve

*It's a ghost.* I probably had a heart attack when Roam went down on me, and I died right there in that changing room.

The only problem was my mom wasn't dead, so she couldn't be a ghost.

Fine, there had to be another explanation. Maybe humans weren't meant to taste a djinn's cake batter, and I was hallucinating.

"Oh my!" My mother covered her eyes and spun around. "I'm so sorry, Genie! Take your time! I'm going to run down to the bakery to get some breakfast."

I remained unmoving, staring at the empty doorway and my hand still frozen around his erection.

"Genevieve." Roam's voice seemed a thousand miles away. "I could take away her memory of this."

When I didn't respond, he sat up, pulling me onto his lap. "Would that make you happy?"

I blinked, bringing his face into focus. My spiraling brain latched onto the way he'd worded his question. He knew I wouldn't wish for it, so he'd worded his question to confirm what I wanted.

Burying my face in my hands, I groaned. "No. I don't want you messing around in my mom's memories. What if you accidentally sent her memories of having a daughter to the same place you sent my boxes?"

"It will be okay, my love," Roam chuckled, rocking me in his arms. "So now what?"

I sighed and dropped my hands to my lap. "You need to brace yourself."

"Is she going to be mad that we had sex before marriage? Or is she going to be mad that you're with a djinn?"

"Neither. You'll see." I decided I would let him figure this one out on his own.

"Then I guess we need to get ready to face her." Roam stood and carried me into the shower.

"You're spoiling me," I murmured as a bubbly sponge smelling of my favorite orange body wash appeared in his hand.

"I enjoy it." He moved the sponge over my skin.

"Thank you," I whispered.

We remained in silence while he shifted our positions and washed my back. When he finished, I reached for the sponge. I rinsed it out and added more soap.

"My turn." I smiled and made soft circles with the sponge on his ethereal blue skin.

"You still refuse to wish for anything."

I kissed a non-soapy spot on his chest. "Because I have everything I could want."

"But you could wish for things to make life easier, upgrade your computer, get a pay raise, or go on a shopping spree." His gaze was so intent I thought it might be burning holes through me. "Why?"

I bit the inside of my cheek. "Can't you read it in my thoughts?"

"I've caught a few thoughts, but I still don't fully understand." Roam pulled me to him, and I tried to ignore how amazing it felt to be held while water ran down our slick bodies.

"When I first awakened you, I didn't want to wish for anything because it seemed wrong. You didn't choose to be a djinn, or to be stuck in a lamp and at the mercy of whoever happened to rub it." I traced his jawline with my fingertips. "Then I started having feelings for you. I never want you to question if my feelings are true or if I simply wanted you for what you could give me."

One minute we were standing under the shower spray, and the next I was completely dry. My back bounced on the bed, and a heartbeat later, Roam's body appeared above me, pressing me into the mattress.

I caught my breath at his glowing eyes. "Roam, your eyes. They've changed again," I whispered. "Why do they do that?"

"Extreme emotion." He placed kisses on my lips, my cheeks, my neck, and my shoulders.

I closed my eyes, savoring every spark and butterfly his touch stirred. He made me feel safe and loved. All my fears about being hurt melted away. I trusted him.

Gripping his hips with my legs and hooking my arms around his neck, I flipped him onto his back.

*Okay, fine.*

He read my mind and rolled over, so that I straddled his stomach.

I caught his face between my palms. "Roam, I know this is way too fast and I have a habit of falling in love easily, but this is different. You aren't like anyone I've ever met—"

"Of course I'm not. I'm a nearly seven-feet-tall blue-skinned djinn," Roam grinned.

"That has nothing to do with it," I scowled, then bit my lip. "Although I'm not complaining."

He brushed his thumb across my bottom lip. "I can change myself to please you better. You only need to tell me."

My heart broke. "I don't need, or want, you to change anything about yourself. You are perfect." I bent to place a soft kiss on his lips. "Roam, I love you. Please don't feel like you have to say it back, because you don't—"

"I wanted you from the moment you touched my lamp. But I started falling in love from our first kiss and the first time I heard your laugh." Roam's lips captured mine in a kiss that left my insides quivering. "I love you."

Resting my head on his chest, I listened to his heartbeat and basked in the love he was radiating.

"I reserve the right to change things to please you. You can't deny you liked the tongue trick," Roam teased.

My body flushed from head to toe. I had enjoyed that, and I was more than a little curious about what he had in mind. "Only if you do it because you want to. You are more than capable of pleasing me without changing a thing."

That brought me to another question I'd been wanting to ask. "Roam, do you want to be free of your lamp and of granting wishes? I can research it and try to find a way."

"It can be done. I discovered another djinn who fell in love with a human. But I don't want that." Roam's hand rubbed circles on my back.

"Why not? I don't ever want you to feel trapped with me." I rubbed his chest.

"Because I like being a djinn. I enjoy the freedom of being able to use my magic to surprise you... and please you. Why do I need to be freed if I'm already free and happy?"

I searched his eyes, looking for any sign that he was lying. But I saw only sincerity. "If you ever change your mind—"

Roam huffed. "You will be the first to know. But that isn't going to happen. And if you change your mind about making wishes, just know I am eager to grant them. I've never granted wishes for someone I loved."

We lay there in silence, just enjoying each other's company.

"Can this work between us?" I whispered.

"This will work." Roam ran his fingers through my hair. "Because we love each other. Now, your mother will be back any minute. Should we prepare to face her?"

Rolling off his chest and onto my back, I groaned into my hands. I knew what was coming, and for a moment, I considered wishing us to be anywhere else in the world. But that would only be putting off the inevitable.

WHEN MY MOM opened the front door, Roam and I were sitting at the table sipping coffee. Despite my embarrassment, I was happy to see her. Standing, I rushed over to hug her.

Roam appeared at her side and took the donut boxes from mom's hands so she could hug me back. "Let me get those for you."

He headed toward the kitchen with them, giving us the illusion of privacy. With a partner who could read my thoughts, there wasn't any real privacy. Some people might have been freaked out or even upset about it, but I loved knowing he was just a thought a way, and that he cared enough to enjoy listening to my nonsensical ramblings so he could get to know me better.

I could admit I was a bit clingy, and having him in my head was a level of closeness I could have only dreamed of.

"Did you have fun?" Mom's stage-whisper brought me back to reality.

"Mom!" I pretended to be angry. "Why are you here? And how did you get inside my house?"

"Sweetie, you've hidden your spare house key inside that creepy cat gnome since you rented your first condo. I think you need a new hiding spot." My mother had the audacity to chuckle. "After our call, I thought I needed to pop in and make sure you didn't run this man off. I'm your mother; I can't help but worry you're going to die alone surrounded by a hundred cats if someone didn't remind you that men exist and they can add a lot to your life."

Her warm green eyes slid toward Roam. "Although based on what I saw, you don't need any help remembering."

I rolled my eyes and led her into the kitchen. "Come meet Roam. My *boyfriend*."

Mom clapped her hands in glee, then grabbed Roam in a hug. "She's stubborn about admitting her feelings, but she's worth the challenge."

Roam stiffened, then relaxed and patted her back. "I'm not going anywhere unless your daughter tries to give me away again."

"ROAM!" I yelped.

"GENIE!" Mom yelled. "You tried to give him away?" Her voice dropped. "Based on what I glimpsed in your bedroom, you need to put a ring on him. Men aren't made like him."

"Mom," I groaned, closing my eyes and briefly considering making a wish for the ground to open up and swallow me.

She lifted her chin and sniffed. "I swear I looked away, but it was kinda too big to miss. No wonder you sounded like you were being strangled."

The sly smirk she shot me didn't go unnoticed by Roam, who bit his lip to keep from laughing.

I sagged down in one of the kitchen table chairs. This was exactly what I thought would happen. My mom had a wicked sense of humor and would do just about anything to see me happy. Over the years, I'd had coworkers with meddling mothers who just wanted grandkids, and pushed hard for them to get married and procreate.

As uncomfortable as this was, my mom's intentions were far different. She knew me as well as I knew myself, and she'd helped me put the pieces of my life back together after having my love thrown in my face. But while my gut reaction was to protect my heart by never falling in love again, she knew that was me denying a huge part of what made me who I was. Mom wanted me to be loved because she knew it was what I needed to be complete.

"Oh! I got you something!" Mom grinned and rushed toward one of the bakery boxes. "Go sit, Roam. This is for you too."

My eyes widened in horror and my heart stopped.

Roam sat and pulled me into his arms. "You look scared, as though you think she's got a viper in that box."

"It's far worse." I licked my dry lips.

"You know what's in the box?" Roam asked, kissing my cheek.

"No, but I know my mom." His hand rested on my stomach and I laced my fingers through his, holding him tight. "Promise you won't run."

"Not a chance," Roam assured me.

Mom sat the box on the table and spun it to face us. "I thought we needed something to celebrate."

Then she lifted the lid, displaying the large cookie cake. A large hot dog had been drawn in icing, and above it was written:

*HOT DOG! You did it!*

*Congrats!*

Roam burst out laughing while I stared slack-jaw at the cookie. I jumped when Mom pulled the string on a tiny plastic champagne bottle.

Mom frowned. "Well, crap. It was supposed to send confetti all over the place. I guess it was a dud."

"Let me help," Roam grinned, and with a snap of his fingers, sparking confetti rained down on the room.

"This is amazing!" Mom cheered, then picked a piece of the confetti up off the table and began laughing so hard she had to sit down.

Glancing down at the table, I stared at the tiny hot dog-shaped confetti.

"Don't encourage her!" I warned him, trying hard not to laugh at the absurdity of the situation.

Roam high-fived my mom. "I think we're going to get along just fine."

"As long as the only thing you break is her bed, and not her heart, we'll get along swimmingly." Mom wiped tears of laughter from her eyes. "Now grab some plates and let's eat. Not all of us had breakfast in bed this morning."

I dropped my head forward, and would have banged it on the table if Roam hadn't slid his hand in the way. Mom never stayed more than two or three days, but I was sure they would be long and hard.

"That's exactly what I'm hoping for," Roam purred against my ear.

# CHAPTER 12

## roam

I thought there would only be one human I liked, and I would learn to tolerate the rest. But Flo, Genie's mom, was a treasure.

She'd offered to go sightseeing on her own to give us privacy, but instead, the three of us had spent the day exploring the island together. I found myself impressed by the number of innuendos Flo managed to work into casual conversation just to embarrass Genie. The bond between the mother and daughter was something special.

As much as I liked Flo, what I enjoyed most had been the way Genie couldn't keep her hands off me. Now that she had opened her heart, she no longer held herself back from showing affection.

At times, her thoughts told me she worried I would become overwhelmed, but that couldn't be further from the truth. After centuries spent alone, I couldn't get enough of being touched and touching her. Sex was mind-blowing, but I equally loved holding her hand, having her rest her head on my chest or shoulder, and feeling her fingers mindlessly rubbing circles on my back.

Last night, we kissed and made out a little, but we hadn't gone all the way. We were enjoying exploring each other's bodies and allowing the anticipation to build. I wanted to claim her body in every way possible, but if she never wanted to take it to the next step, it wouldn't change how I felt.

Swiping the sweat from my brow, I turned slowly around the yard, checking that I hadn't missed any of the bushes and that the grass was perfectly trimmed.

Flo bustled outside, carrying a glass of lemonade. "Roam, you're going to end up dehydrated if you don't stop to drink."

"Thank you, Flo." I lifted the glass, draining it in seconds.

"You can call me Mom." She grinned at me, then with her hands on her hips, she surveyed the yard. "What are you doing out here? And why don't you just use magic instead of exhausting yourself in this heat?"

"I could've used magic, but as idiotic as it sounds, I'm enjoying doing things with my hands. Working makes the time away from Genie pass faster." I hesitated, not sure how honest to be with Flo about my sudden interest in yard work.

Remembering the bag of massage oils and candles she'd

given us as a second housewarming present, I decided it was fine to be blunt. "Genie can't focus well during intimacy if the yard is out of control. I enjoy sharing that with your daughter, so I wanted to make sure she wasn't stressed."

Flo's forehead creased. "That's strange. Genie has never had a green thumb or cared about plants other than roses. What exactly did she say?"

"We were in the middle of"—I hesitated—"kissing, and she started worrying. Her exact thought was she needed to check into permanent ways to keep the bush cleared away and the landscape smooth. I will do anything to keep her from feeling anxious when she should feel amazing, so I've cleared away all the bushes, and the grass is all the same length. I've checked it twice."

"I see." Flo's cheeks turned red, and she covered her mouth with her hand.

"My apologies. Considering your constant teasing and encouragement of our physical relationship, I didn't realize my honesty would be embarrassing." I scratched the back of my neck.

"No, no. It's not that, sweet boy!" Tears leaked from Flo's eyes and her shoulders began to shake. "I can assure you my daughter isn't worried about her lawn, although I know she is going to appreciate the work you put in to please her."

She barely got the words out before she burst into laughter and headed back toward the house. "Genie is going to be tickled over this."

I was missing something, but I couldn't figure out what. Oh well, Genie would explain it later.

There were several more hours before she returned home, and I decided that was plenty of time to make three overdue house calls.

I suspected Genie wouldn't like it if I straight up killed her exes, but that didn't mean I couldn't have a little fun while making them pay for every single tear they'd caused her to cry. They wouldn't be dead, but they wouldn't be very happy about being alive either.

# CHAPTER 13

## genevieve

"Checking your watch again? I'm starting to think you can't wait to get away from us." Tiny laughed at the blush staining my cheeks.

"That's not true! I love working with all of you!" I hurried to protest.

"I bet it's because of that sexy piece of man candy she brought to the festival. That man never took his eyes off her!" Bitzy laughed and dodged the pen I threw at her.

"I'm surprised she can talk with the way he makes her scream." Barker joined in the banter and I stuck my tongue out at the fairy, which she playfully returned as she headed back toward the reception desk.

Frost closed his laptop. "Well, good news, Vi. It's time to head home to your lover boy." He threw his backpack over his shoulder and winked at me as he passed.

"Hang on, we'll walk out with you!" Bitzy called after him as she and Tiny gathered their things.

"Be sure to get at least a couple hours of sleep tonight," my cryptid coworker whispered as she and Tiny hurried past me to catch up.

"I can't wait until you start dating someone and I can return all this teasing!" I shouted after her.

She gave me a single finger salute, then blew me a kiss over her shoulder. Shaking my head, I closed my laptop and started tucking my personal items into my shoulder bag.

As I headed past the reception desk, I noticed Barker was still sitting in front of the screen. Her usually bright, cheerful face appeared stressed.

"Everything okay, B?" I changed course and headed toward the desk.

"It's fine. Just my computer seems to have taken a client spreadsheet and mangled it beyond repair. If I can't fix it, I'll have to cancel my girls' weekend and spend hours gathering the information from scratch so I have it in time for Monday's presentation." She looked up at me, and I could see her eyes were red.

"You've been crying!" I placed my bag on the desktop and moved around to take the spare chair beside her. "I'm pretty good with spreadsheets. Let's take a look at it real quick."

Barker hesitated. "Are you sure? I know you're excited to head home."

"I'm sure! This probably won't take more than a half hour to fix. Now scoot over and let me get in here."

Barker threw her arms around my neck. "You're the best! I'll owe you one!"

It took exactly thirty-four minutes to restore the jumbled spreadsheet to its original glory. I still couldn't figure out how her computer had managed to mangle it so badly. Heck, half of it hadn't even been in English.

I wiggled in the backseat of the taxi as we turned onto my street. My heart pounded and my hands trembled in anticipation. Would I ever get used to arriving home to Roam? I doubted it.

HOPPING out of the car before it had even come to a full stop, I thanked the driver and rushed up the sidewalk. My excitement turned to unease as I noticed the house was dark.

The sun was low enough on the horizon that they normally would have the lights on inside the house. Maybe Mom and Roam decided to grill out back and were waiting for me to join them. Yes, that was it.

Excitement bubbled in my chest and I picked up my pace.

All hope that things were okay vanished when I reached for the door handle and found the door wasn't latched. Not sure what I was going to find, and wanting to be able to move quickly if needed to, I lowered my bag onto the porch and silently kicked off my heels.

I cautiously pushed the door open and stepped inside. The setting sun cast its light onto the destroyed interior of the house.

My dining table had been flipped, and pieces of the chairs were scattered about the room. The few decorations I'd brought from the mainland lay shattered on the floor. Glitter sparkled all over the room, causing bile to rise in my throat, choking me.

Things could be replaced. But where were my mother and Roam? He wouldn't have allowed this type of damage to my house unless he'd been injured... or worse.

A soft thud came from the kitchen. It grew louder, repeating over and over.

*Thud, thud, thud.*

I kept close to the wall as I moved soundlessly toward the noise. It was coming from my pantry. Grabbing a knife from the sink, I crept closer and flung open the door.

"MOM!" I gasped, dropping to my knees.

Ropes were tied around her ankles, and her wrists were tied behind her back. Yanking the kitchen dishcloth from her mouth, I fought panic.

"Are you hurt?" I was surprised that instead of tears, I felt anger.

The moment her wrists were free, mom batted my hands away. "Stop that! I'm fine! A little stiff, but no lasting damage. They snuck up on Roam. I heard him shout and hurried in here to find him collapsed on the floor. The next thing I know, something hit the back of my head and I don't remember much else."

"You said they? Did you see them?" I demanded, my fingernails digging into my palms.

"I only saw a man, but I thought I heard a second voice. Is Roam okay?" She peered out of the closet, searching for him.

"I haven't checked upstairs, but I didn't see any sign of him down here. If you're okay, I'm going to go search for him."

"Go, hurry!" she ordered.

Leaping to my feet, I ran up the stairs, searching the two rooms and bathrooms. He was nowhere to be found. Rushing back downstairs, I ran to the bookshelf for his lamp, hoping maybe he'd disappeared inside it to heal from an injury or something.

I skidded to a stop and felt my blood turn to ice as I stared at the empty shelf. They'd taken Roam and his lamp.

Stumbling back toward the pantry, I sagged to the floor beside my mom. My mind spun as my world collapsed. I was a graphic designer, not a secret agent or a paranormal with special abilities. The truth was, I didn't even know how to start looking for him.

My first guess would have been Linda. She clearly wanted the lamp for her collection, which made me think maybe it had a high monetary value, but why would she take Roam? Plus, mom said a man had been the one to tie her up.

My eyes drifted to the ropes that had been used to

restrain my mom. No, they weren't ropes. They were lime green bungee cords.

I didn't own a set of bungee cords, which meant the kidnapper had brought the cords with him. Did that mean this was a professional job? What if Linda hired someone to break in and steal the lamp so she didn't have to get her hands dirty? Maybe Roam had seen their faces and they couldn't risk leaving him behind and telling the police.

Rushing to the porch, I dug my phone out of my handbag. I unlocked the screen and pressed it into mom's hand. "Call the cops. Get them here and an ambulance to check you out."

With that, I bolted toward the front door and dashed down the street. Linda said she'd moved into the neighborhood and had motioned toward the homes that sat in the less populated part of the subdivision.

My bare feet pounded against the sandy asphalt as I ran down the sidewalk. I didn't have a plan, and I knew what I was doing was stupid. But I didn't care. The need to do something—anything—to find Roam drove me forward.

I scanned each house, searching for anything that stood out or a sign of Linda. It was the truck parked in front of the last house on the street that caused me to stumble to a stop.

My mind flashed to the day I'd moved into my house. I'd sat on a stack of boxes watching the movers unpack my furniture and carry it into the house. Furniture they'd secured in the moving truck using lime green bungee cords.

How were the movers involved with Linda? Dropping to a

crouch, I ran along the fence-line toward the moving van. I reached the driver's side door first and opened it. It didn't take long to search the truck and confirm the lamp wasn't there.

I did find a box cutter, and slipped it into my pocket. It would have been smarter to bring the giant knife from the kitchen, but nothing about my race to find Roam had been well-planned. I was the chick who would die at the beginning of the movie for doing something stupid, like running straight into a creepy murder workshop or taking a shortcut through a graveyard.

Moving to the back of the truck, I found the liftgate was open. But the truck was empty.

Except for a thin layer of familiar purple dust. Roam had been there. So where was he now?

Looking at the ground, I caught the glint of purple dust. It led around the side of the house, through the fence and onto a stone patio that surrounded an empty pool that was still under construction.

A murmur of voices drifted across the backyard. Staying close to the fence, I moved toward them while straining to hear what was being said.

"You swore to me if we did this, I would get what was supposed to be mine," a deep male voice rumbled. "You can't change it just because your golden child throws a tantrum."

A woman's voice responded, but I wasn't close enough to hear.

"You can't allow this, Mom!" a shrill voice cut through

the silence. "He can wait for the next djinn lamp to fix whatever screws are loose with his power."

"You would screw me over just because you're desperate to screw a guy you barely know?" The male's voice rose, trembling with rage. "The only reason you want him is because you're jealous of her! Admit it!"

I peeked around a tall, perfectly sculpted hedge, finally catching sight of the speakers. The world wobbled wildly and the roar of rushing blood filled my ears. It couldn't be.

My mind replayed every event since I'd arrived on the island. What was it she had said?

*"I'm surprised she can talk with the way he makes her scream."*

How did she know Roam had made me scream?

The only time I'd been vocal outside of the house was in the changing room. Roam had assured me he had magically soundproofed it because he'd planned to make me scream his name, and he hadn't wanted someone bursting in to save me.

I watched in horror as she smirked, twirling the lamp in her hand. "Well, Mom's magic forced him back in the lamp, which means the moment I rub this, he's mine."

"Barker, don't you dare," Charles hissed. "I've spent years searching for a djinn lamp. I found this one, and it's mine."

"Better luck next time, big bro." She pretended to frown, then gave a cruel laugh that twisted her sweet fairy features into a grotesque mask.

I was already racing across the ground when she brought her palm toward the side of the lamp.

She was not about to take my man.

It didn't matter that she was a paranormal, and I was a human armed with nothing more than a box cutter. I was about to send her sparkly self straight to Hades.

*I wonder how they feel about people who glitter bomb the afterlife.*

# CHAPTER 14

## genevieve

I barreled into Barker with a fury far worse than that of a stampeding bull—the fury of a woman in love who is unhinged enough to die protecting her man. It was likely the shock of having me appear out of nowhere and screaming like a banshee that kept Linda, Charles and Barker frozen in place.

My body collided with Barker's smaller one, sending us both flying backward. We toppled over the piles of dirt and into the empty pool, where our bodies crashed hard into the ground.

Rocks dug into various parts of my body, and I knew I'd be rocking a giraffe print pattern on my skin the next day, but I was too angry to feel any pain. Not giving her a chance to process what had happened, I scrambled toward the lamp.

Everything would be fine if I could just get to Roam.

"I don't think so, human," Barker spat, leaping onto my back. Her weight threw me off balance and sent us slamming hard into the ground a second time. "He's mine."

"Roam isn't an item you can claim like a pair of new shoes!" I bit down on her arm and brought my knee up hard into her midsection.

Barker shrieked in pain and rolled off me. "Djinn do as they're told."

I threw myself toward the lamp that lay less than six feet away. Seeing what I had planned, Barker launched herself at it too.

My fingers were less than an inch from the lamp when lightning struck me. I curled into the fetal position, screaming in agony as my muscles convulsed.

"I tried to get the lamp from you nicely, but you just had to be stubborn." Linda stood at the edge of the pool, looking down at me with disgust, smoke curling from her hand. "See where your greediness got you?"

"My greediness? You're the one breaking and entering to steal something that doesn't belong to you and attacking two people who did nothing to you." Each word hurt like heck to speak, but I refused to die a sobbing mess.

Linda waved her hand dismissively. "We didn't know your mother was visiting, and the djinn is too rare an artifact to be left in the hands of humans. That power needs to stay within the paranormal community."

Charles dropped down into the hole.

I scowled up at him as he approached. "And what part do you play in this?"

"I saw you unbox the lamp while moving your furniture inside the house and knew immediately what it was. If I could have snatched it right then, I would have, but I thought it would be child's play to get it from you later. Except you refused to invite me home. You were willing to sleep with a djinn, but not me?" Charles' eyes rolled over my skin with a look I didn't like.

I should've let him stay dead.

Charles puffed out his chest. "I'm the son of a warlock and an enchantress. You should feel honored to have me show you any attention at all."

"Yeah, a lame one born without magic." Barker curled her lip in disgust. "Mom had the dud first. Then married a fairy and had me. I wasn't involved in Charles and mom's scheme. Not until the rose festival. They wanted me to distract you so they could dart the djinn with a cocktail capable of taking down a paranormal."

She picked up the lamp, dangling it by the handle from one finger. "I did my part, but then, thanks to a weird quirk of being half fairy and half enchantress, I caught a glimpse of his figure in the dunking booth. As if that wasn't enough, later, I walked by the changing room and heard his voice. I heard the way you screamed, and I knew I wanted to experience a lover like that. And now I will."

"That's creepy. Do you lurk around listening to everyone have sex? Maybe if you put more effort into your own sex life, you wouldn't have to be envious of mine." I pretended to gag.

She held up the lamp, watching to see if I would lunge

for her, but I couldn't. The muscles in my legs and arms refused to obey my commands.

"It belongs to me!" Charles roared, rushing at Barker. "I won't let you ruin this!"

He was so much larger than Barker, and I was expecting him to flatten her, but she rolled her eyes and flung him into the wall with a flick of her hand. Charles didn't stay down long, and a heartbeat later, he sprung toward her with his hands outstretched.

Another flick of her wrist sent him crashing into a cement mixer that sat at the far side of the hole. The unmistakable sound of bones cracking was followed by a groan from Charles. Still, he pushed back to his feet, staggering slightly.

A trickle of blood ran from his temple down his cheek. "Mother! Help me! This isn't what we agreed on."

We all stared up at Linda, who stood at the edge of the hole. Her brow was creased, and she glanced back and forth between her two unhinged offspring.

"If you raise a finger against me, I'll tell Dad. What do you think the fairy courts will think of you using magic against me?" The smugness in Barker's tone had Linda's eye twitching. Clearly, I wasn't the only one who wanted to knock some sense into the self-centered, cruel fairy.

Linda's fists clenched and unclenched at her sides.

"Mother! Who knows how long before we locate another djinn? If we don't use this one to complete the spell, I may never reach my full potential," Charles pleaded.

Barker watched the unfolding drama with cool amusement. "Give it up. If she uses her magic against me, she'll be forfeiting her life. Fairy code dictates it, and she became a citizen of the fairy courts when she married Dad."

Charles' face darkened with rage, and if I could have moved, I would have backed away from him.

Barker fake yawned. "You don't even know if it would have worked. So stop getting so worked up."

"It would! My vessel is strong, built to handle magic. The spell will allow me to absorb the djinn, and his magic will become mine."

My stomach pitched, and I fought the urge to vomit. What was wrong with them? How could they talk about him as though he were a commodity and nothing more than an object to possess for their selfish desires?

"Bro, quit hanging onto Mom's lies," Barker snorted. "You see, I did a little snooping around about that spell. It did a number on my computer and messed up a bunch of documents. You might want to do a DNA test. Let's just say, I think Mom decided to do a little dumpster diving in her younger years and she seemed to have a thing for humans. The spell works in theory, but it has killed everyone who has used it."

Charles' mouth opened and closed as he stared in disbelief at Linda.

Barker's eyes cut to me and she whispered, "Thanks for helping fix that, by the way. I was supposed to stop you from leaving until they stopped by your house. My plan was to knock you out and lock you in the bathroom for the weekend, but you were so nice to offer to help me, and that slowed you down."

"You know," I wheezed, trying to breathe through the fiery pain radiating through every fiber of my muscles. "The more I get to know my co-workers, the better I understand why Noah only let animals join him on the ark."

"I compliment you and you act like that?" Barker kicked out her foot, landing a solid blow to my cheek.

Agonizing pain stabbed my skull, and a copper taste burst across my tongue as my vision blurred.

"Do you have something else to say, Vivi?"

Refusing to let her see how much pain I was in, I spat the blood from my mouth. "Yeah. I hope the love of your life gets stuck in a condom."

Was it smart to goad a lunatic? No.

Did it hurt like a son-of-a-biscuit-eater when her cute pink boot hit my shoulder with enough force to dislocate it with a sickening pop? Oh, yeah.

Was the rage on her face worth it? Without a doubt.

Seeing she was distracted, Charles rushed her. This time, he made contact, sending them both tumbling into the wall. Charles wrapped his hands around her throat, and I thought he might actually win. Then she threw out her hand, and I watched in horror as a piece of metal rebar flew to her hand as though she held a magnet.

Barker didn't even hesitate before plunging it through Charles' chest. He stared down at the crimson stain blossoming on his chest.

"Ugh!" Barker groaned, heaving him off her and

standing without even sparing him another glance. "I was basically saving his life by not giving him what he wanted, and the only thanks I get are bloodstains on my vintage blouse. Oh well, the djinn will fix it."

Over my dead body. I focused on my rage, willing it to give me the strength to get up and fight.

"Charles!" Linda landed softly in the dirt. "Barker! He's your brother. How could you?"

"Relax. Once the djinn is mine, I'll wish for him to heal your precious firstborn. But if you try to stop me, it will be too late."

Linda looked torn between grabbing for the lamp herself, or letting Barker have her way. At last, she dropped her head. "I won't stop you. Please hurry."

The woman was off her rocker if she thought Barker would keep her word. One look at the fairy's face made it clear she found Charles' death of no more importance than that of a fly.

Barker moved to stand in front of me, no doubt wanting to make sure I was watching as she took the most important thing in the world from me. She maintained eye contact and smirked as she lifted her hand and rubbed the lamp.

My heart broke, and I braced myself for the pain I was going to experience when he was forced to answer her summons. He'd be bound to obey her.

I waited for the familiar sparkling dust to appear, but nothing happened.

Barker cursed, rubbing harder at the lamp.

Yet again, no sparks nor clouds of swirling purple appeared.

"Even if he answers the summons, you will never have him as your lover. Djinn have to grant wishes, but they can't be forced into sharing their bodies. They have to choose to give it." I took an incredible amount of pleasure in telling her that little fact. "Roam loves me, and you'll never get to experience how incredible it is to have him as a lover."

"Lies!" Barker screeched, rubbing harder and harder at the lamp.

Still, nothing happened.

I was equal parts terrified and relieved. Maybe our bond was strong enough that he was able to resist her. But what if the reason Roam wasn't answering was because he was gravely injured or worse?

"Tell me how to summon him!" Barker's open palm smacked my swollen face.

"Never." I clenched my jaw.

Barker's face turned a deeper shade of purple than Roam's eyes. "You can delay all you want, but he will be mine. Even if I have to bring your mom down here and force you to transfer ownership in exchange for her life."

Instead of focusing on my rage, I focused on how Roam made me feel and the intensity of the love I felt for him.

My muscles twitched, my control slowly returning.

*It's about freaking time.*

With herculean effort, I pushed myself into a sitting position. "I can't do that."

"You can and you will!" Barker shrieked, rubbing furiously at the lamp, to no avail.

I swayed, but righted myself. "You have it all wrong. It's Roam who owns me."

Reaching into my pocket, I pulled out the box cutter. Between my blurred vision and the darkening twilight, I struggled to see my target clearly.

The box cutter wouldn't do fatal damage, but Barker's vanity would work to my advantage. I had one shot at this.

"Fine, I'll tell you how," I whispered, dropping my head forward.

Barker fell for my act and squatted in front of me. "I knew you'd give in."

Lifting my head, I stared straight into her cruel eyes. "Oh, wait. I forgot I don't explain myself to idiots."

With a speed I would definitely brag to Roam about later, I slashed the box cutter across her face, trying to make the cut as long as possible.

"My face!" Barker reacted exactly how I thought she would—concern over her face having a scar distracting her from all of us.

I reached for the lamp, but before I could do more than touch it with the tip of my finger, a bolt of electricity, much like the one that had hit me, hit the lamp.

"If I can't have him, then you can't either!" Barker's eyes were wild with a feral rage as she blasted the lamp with her magic.

"Barker, NO!" Linda screamed, raising her hands and sending a burst of magic at her daughter.

It distracted the fairy, and she turned her magic on her mother.

I scrambled to the lamp, sobbing as I saw the melted metal of the lamp spreading like cooling lava across the ground. The intricate etchings were gone, and if I hadn't known what it had been just a minute before, I'd never have guessed it was once a lamp.

From somewhere behind me, I heard Barker's harsh laugh. "I guess no one is going to win today."

Purple dust coated the ground. I gathered it in my hands, sobbing harder when I realized it no longer sparkled. It was little more than ash.

He was gone.

I'd lost him.

Burying my fingers in the dust, I cried for the man who'd shown me true love. Now that I'd had a taste of it, I couldn't imagine being able to survive a single day without it.

"All those times you wanted to grant a wish for me, and now that I finally want to make a wish, you're gone." I knew he was gone, and I sounded crazy, but this was the only opportunity I'd have to say my goodbyes. "Roam, I wish you were with me. I told you I was going to cling to you like an octopus and never let you get away. I wish that was possible in the real world—not the octopus part—but the being tied together for the rest of my life."

Darkness had fallen and the only sound was my sobs. Muscles weak, I dropped to my side on the ground. And there, curled up in the midst of the purple dust, I screamed at the unfairness of it all.

# CHAPTER 15

## roam

I was floating in the vast emptiness of unconsciousness, completely disembodied. Whatever the enchantress had injected me with was keeping me drugged and confused.

Pain flickered like lightning through the darkness enveloping me. I was in my lamp, which meant I couldn't feel pain. But if the pain didn't belong to me… where did it come from?

*I hope the love of your life gets stuck in a condom.*

The feminine voice was defiant.

This time, when the pain crackled through the darkness, it brought the taste of blood.

My frustration grew as I tried to sort through the fog of my confusion. Djinn couldn't experience pain inside the safety of our lamps, and we didn't know what was going on outside our lamps until summoned.

Wait. That wasn't completely true. Or was it?

No, I'd felt something—someone—outside of the lamp before.

The soft stumbling of my heart beginning to beat echoed in the darkness. It was yet one more thing I shouldn't be experiencing in the empty. I had no need for a heart when I didn't have a body.

Something touched the lamp, and my purple magic glowed in response. Was I being summoned?

*Roam loves me and you'll never get to experience how incredible it is to have him as a lover.*

The fog vanished in the blink of an eye.

*Genie.* My joy at hearing her voice quickly turned to an all-consuming rage. If that was Genie's voice I was hearing, was it her pain I felt, and her blood I tasted?

My magic expanded and contracted like a living, breathing thing. But it was useless; I couldn't escape the confines of the lamp.

Had the enchantress been smart enough to cast a spell that trapped me in the lamp until summoned? That was the only thing that made sense.

Someone rubbed the lamp harder, and my magic swirled in response, preparing to fulfill the only purpose I had: granting wishes.

No, that wasn't true. I had a different purpose now that fulfilled me more than granting thousands of wishes ever had.

Cuddling Genie, learning to cook for her, finding new

ways to make her moan, and figuring out what made her eyes sparkle.

I existed to love her, and that wasn't her touch trying to summon me. Recoiling from the foreign touch, I used the strength of the love Genie had showered me with to ignore the summons—something that should have been impossible for a djinn.

There was nothing I wanted more than to be free from the lamp, but if I answered the summons, I would be at the new owner's whims. My magic, my body, and my heart belonged to Genie. I'd die rather than allow someone to force us apart.

*You have it all wrong. It's Roam who owns me.*

I bellowed in anguish and fury. Genie was scared and in pain, yet she was declaring to the world that she was owned by a djinn. It went against the world's belief that djinn weren't like other species and our only reason for being was to serve.

It wasn't just fear and pain I sensed through our tenuous connection. She was proud to be mine.

Whoever was trying to summon me became frantic, and the swirling magic rushed to answer. The command may have been strong, but my love for Genie was stronger.

Closing my eyes, I listened for the soft beat of my heart and began spinning the magic tighter and tighter around it. I strained against the will of whoever was trying to force me out.

Just when I thought I might not have the strength to resist, I felt Genie through the bond. She was reaching for the love we shared with a desperation that terrified me. It gave me the strength I needed to keep fighting.

*Fine, I'll tell you how.*

Her words signaled defeat, but I could still sense the determination. What was she planning?

The rubbing ceased.

*I forgot I don't explain myself to idiots.*

Unexpected laughter bubbled from me. *That's my girl.*

Whoever had the lamp must have dropped it, because my world began flipping end over end.

For a heartbreakingly brief second, Genie touched the interior of the lamp, banishing the darkness and bathing me in the warmth of her love.

Then she was gone.

*NO!* I screamed, my world plunging back into miserable darkness.

Magic blasted the outside of the lamp. It wasn't dark magic, nor was it more powerful than my magic when I was free. But trapped inside the lamp, there was little I could do but throw my magic against the walls trapping me inside as I tried to get to Genie. Whatever spell had been used to keep me from using her original summons to escape held firm.

As the ancient djinn etchings melted away, my swirling magic flickered and dimmed. My heartbeat slowed until it finally beat its last.

The lamp was being destroyed, and a djinn couldn't exist without that anchor. Maybe I should have let Genie wish for me to become human, but I liked being a djinn and didn't want to change.

It had been freeing to have a woman who showed me every day that she loved me exactly how I was. For the first time in my very long life, I'd gotten to be me and it had felt amazing.

I'd gotten a taste of what it was like to be alive, and now I was dying.

The only thing I wished was that I'd gotten the chance to tell her I loved her one last time.

As the blast of magic vanished, my magic drifted across the earth, useless as ash. I couldn't see anything, but I felt the cool night air, which confirmed what I already knew. I was no longer inside my lamp.

Clinging to the last fading sparks of the magic that had made me what I was, I strained to hear her voice just one more time.

Something brushed against the last flickering ember of magic.

*Genie.*

Her tears broke me. I'd promised I wouldn't hurt her, but now she was sobbing over a broken heart.

"All those times you wanted to grant a wish for me, and now that I finally want to make a wish, you're gone."

She was right; I'd wanted to grant a wish for her. I couldn't help it, granting wishes was woven into the fiber of what I was, and using my abilities to please her was exciting.

I longed to grant this wish for her and the ember of

magic my consciousness was clinging to flared in response, but I was too weak. Tears continued raining down around me. I knew what this was. She was telling me goodbye.

"Roam, I wish you were with me. I told you I was going to cling to you like an octopus and never let you get away. I wish that was possible in the real world—not the octopus part—but the being tied together for the rest of my life."

The ember flared again, reaching for her. And when she collapsed on top of my fallen ash, the tiny spark was caught up in the air. It drifted down to land against her skin, where it glowed to life.

The dust touching that single ember began to glow. Then, like dominos, the light spread from spark to spark.

I realized too late what was happening.

Genie had found a loophole, and I wasn't sure how she was going to feel about it.

# CHAPTER 16

## genevieve

I lay with my eyes closed, although thanks to the swelling, I wasn't sure I could open them even if I'd possessed the energy. Every part of my body was in agony, and with each shaking breath I took, fiery pain shot through my dislocated shoulder. But it was nothing compared to the devastation that was laying waste to my heart and soul.

Comforting warmth spread up my leg from my ankle, reminding me of Roam's touch. My body began shaking with fresh sobs. He was gone.

The sweet warmth spread up to my hip, then across my belly. Maybe my mind was creating the illusion to help me cope with the loss. Keeping my eyes closed, I reached for the glow, pretending it was Roam, and he was here with me. That I wasn't alone.

I gasped in shock when the heat picked up speed, racing

across my skin, then sinking deeper until it felt as though my blood pulsed with Roam's magic.

My heart raced and my breathing grew rough. This wasn't in my head. Opening my eyes, as far as the swelling would allow, I found I was no longer in darkness.

Purple dust swirled around me, reminding me of the day Roam had appeared and changed my life. Except it was different. Instead of the single shade of purple, every hue of purple and pink imaginable whirled around me. And the glitter had turned to twinkling stars that glowed as they danced in the air.

"Roam?" I whispered, voice hoarse from my sobs.

*I'm here,* he whispered in my mind. *And better than ever.*

What did that mean? The cloud began flexing and expanding, slowly taking the shape of a man.

My brain flashed to the childhood trauma I'd suffered after a certain sexy beast's glow-up did him dirty and he went from hot to not.

It didn't matter. I'd love Roam no matter what he looked like... worst case, maybe he'd be able to shift forms to the old one I'd fallen in love with occasionally for some bedroom fun.

His laughter came from the cloud, taking my breath away and caressing my aching heart. "I love your strange mind."

With a last flourish, the dust disappeared, leaving the man I loved with my entire being standing over me.

Roam appeared at my side, bending over me and gently wiping the wetness from my cheek.

"I tried to save you. I tried so hard." Tears slid down my cheeks and my throat tightened, this time a mix of regret and relief.

"My love, why did you put yourself through this?" A single tear slid down his cheek. "I felt your pain, and it tore me up, but I knew if I answered the summons, I would be forced to answer to someone else. I refused to live without you, but it broke me."

"And that's why I fought Barker. I love you too much to allow someone to use you. You deserve more," I whispered.

Roam's lips found mine in a kiss that curled my toes and caused my skin to flush, then cool. Surprised, I broke the kiss to touch my face and shoulder. My injuries were gone, and not even a hint of soreness had been left behind. He'd healed me.

"You are my everything. I love you, Roam. Now and forever."

"I love you with my entire being, and there is something I need to tell you." Roam pulled me into his arms.

I glanced toward where the three motionless bodies lay. Linda and Barker had turned their magic on each other, and the vicious burns marring their skin caused my stomach to pitch wildly. "Can we go somewhere else? Please?"

He nodded. "Absolutely."

"Wait!" I sighed. "Mom is probably worried. I need to tell her we're okay. And we should probably call the cops and wait for them to get here before we leave."

"It can wait." Roam stood, cradling me in his arms as though I weighed nothing.

"Crime scenes don't really wait." I chewed my lip, torn between needing to be held and reassured that he was safe, but not wanting to end up looking like the prime suspect in a triple homicide.

"They do if I bend time a bit." He winked at me. "I told you I was better than ever."

The next time I blinked, Roam was gently laying me on my back on a cloudlike comforter. I twisted my neck, trying to see where we were and caught my breath. We were in a cabin in the middle of a snowy dreamscape.

One entire wall of the cabin was glass, allowing me to watch as giant flakes of snow fell, covering the evergreen forest that stretched out in the gently sloping valley below us. The left wall was made entirely of mismatched stones, and held a crackling fire that cast the room in a romantic glow.

"It's beautiful," I whispered.

"I'm glad you like it." His eyes glowed that deep purple that spoke of his love, except they were different.

Catching his face between my hands, I pulled him down until our lips nearly touched. "Roam, there's green in your eyes."

"That's what I need to explain." He gently sucked my bottom lip, then reluctantly released it. "Genie, you made a wish."

My eyes widened. "You heard me?"

He nodded, not quite meeting my eyes. "And so did my magic. I'm not sure how literal you intended your words to be taken, but the djinn magic latched onto them and took it very seriously."

I scrunched up my nose and squinted at him. "Why do you look like that's something bad? You're here with me. I don't care how that happened."

Wrapping my legs around his waist, I pulled his body down on top of me and began kissing his bare chest. He'd nearly died, and I refused to risk it happening again before we had sex. That was a regret I didn't want to live with.

Roam groaned, and I felt his hardness press against me. "Genie, listen. The octopus thing."

"Mm-hm," I murmured, rolling my hips so that our bodies ground together.

"You are making it hard to think," he rasped out.

"Then spit it out quickly so I can feel you inside me. I don't want to wait any longer." I flicked his nipple with my tongue.

"I'm inside you."

I froze. Surely I'd know if he was inside me. Heck, I had very vivid memories of his length and girth in my mouth. Wanting to be sure, I snuck a quick glance between our bodies.

"Not like that," Roam snorted. "Believe me, you'll know when I'm inside you because you'll be screaming my name."

He pulled away from me, sitting up and putting distance between us so he could talk. "I was dying because I was no longer bound to the lamp. You made a wish, and the magic took that, plus your open heart and love, as you offering yourself as my anchor."

"Are you going to go inside me like you did your lamp? I mean, if that's part of the price I have to pay to have you here, I'll learn to deal. But it is a little weird." The mental image of rubbing my belly to make him appear had my lips twitching, even though that was definitely not the time for my weird sense of humor.

"No, the only time I'll be inside you is during sex. The magic is tying us together and flowing between our bodies. You can't use it like I can, but it's weaving through your DNA." He reached out, taking my hand. "Genie, there is no way to undo this without me dying. And because djinn are immortal, as long as I'm bound to you, my magic is going to keep your body from aging."

That took a minute to process. But it didn't matter. I would agree to anything to have the love of my life with me.

Climbing onto his lap, I straddled him. "So what you're saying is you're stuck with me forever?"

Roam's hands slid under my shirt to rest against my bare skin. I shivered.

"Since your magic accepted my offer to be your vessel, and your magic is flowing through me to keep me alive for you…" Another thought occurred to me and I went up on my knees to brush my lips against him, teasing us both. "Does that mean you own me now?"

"We belong to each other." Grabbing my waist, he spun us around and pinned me beneath him.

"Good," I whispered. "You can never leave me. I guess I'll just have to Djinn and bear it."

"Maybe it should be Djinn and *bare* it." Roam laughed and trailed his fingers down my body, causing my clothes to disappear at his touch. It was a nifty trick, as long as he didn't accidentally do it while we were grocery shopping or something.

"My love, nothing but death was ever going to take me. I told you I was yours forever," he chuckled, his hot breath teasing the skin between my breasts. "Tonight just made it official."

Happiness burst inside me. I would never be alone again.

"Enough talking. I'm dying to know what it feels like to have a djinn claim every part of my body as his."

Roam's eyes lit with lust. "You have no idea how much I've thought about this," he whispered, dipping his head to lick and kiss my breast.

"I'm pretty sure I do. In fact, I'm beginning to think I want it more since you seem more interested in talking—" My sarcasm got me exactly what I wanted.

Roam pressed the head of his thick erection against my soaked entrance. He shifted his weight to his left arm to keep from squishing me under his large frame.

His right palm moved to settle on my lower back, just above my butt, and he used it to hold me against him as he slowly pressed inside. I closed my eyes and focused on my breathing as he stretched my tight heat.

My body wasn't accustomed to accepting something of

his size, and despite how slick and aroused I was, it was hard not to squirm away.

Roam stopped moving, holding himself motionless. "My love, you have to relax your muscles."

"It will be fine. You can keep going." I'd been trying not to think about the pain because I didn't want him to know, but the stupid tremble in my voice gave away how uncomfortable I was.

"I won't risk hurting you." Roam placed a sweet kiss on my lips. "I'm going to make it feel better."

I opened my eyes. "No, I want our first time to be with your natural form."

He hesitated, then nodded. "I won't change the size, but I can do other things to increase your pleasure."

A delicious warmth rippled through my aching walls as his thick erection grew hotter. It was like having a heating pad on sore muscles and I immediately moaned in pleasure. When his right hand moved to brush against my clit, I trembled.

Looking at my lover, I took in the tenderness that shone in his eyes as he took care of me as his muscles rippled under the strain of resisting the urge to move inside me.

"You are the sexiest woman to ever walked this earth," he murmured, his eyes never looking away from mine.

"That's what you're supposed to say," I rasped, struggling to think of anything other than the sensations he caused everywhere he kissed and touched.

"It's the truth, Genevieve. You have no idea how hard it

is not to have my hands on you twenty-four hours a day."
His mouth kissed and sucked my needy breasts.

The pleasure of the heat, his finger stimulating me, his
length filling me, and the love I could read in his eyes was
more than I could take. I fell apart, crying out his name.

My hips bucked, and I gasped as it plunged him deep,
hard and fast. Instead of pain, all I felt was pure pleasure.

Roam hissed as though in pain. "Genie. I didn't realize
that was going to happen. You feel even more incredible
than I'd imagined."

I barely heard him. My body had adjusted, and I wanted
more. Rolling my hips against him, we moaned in pleasure.

"Make love to me," I whispered. "I want to be yours in
every way possible."

That was all he needed to hear. Bracing himself on his
elbows, Roam rolled against me, his rhythm sexy and
reminding me of undulating waves. As he pulled back, his
hard length stroked me in ways that had my eyes rolling
back in my head, and then he'd thrust back inside, setting
off an entirely different set of erotic sensation.

Far too quickly, I could feel my release reaching the
point of no return. "Roam."

"Come for me," he commanded.

And I did.

"I love you!" I screamed as he grabbed my hips and
thrust in time with the waves of pleasure crashing
through me.

"It's only because of you I know what love is," he
rasped. "You're squeezing me so tight, I can't hold back—"

His body stiffened and he wrapped an arm under me, holding me to him as he twitched inside me.

When he caught his breath, he kissed my lips and whispered, "I love you."

Every little move was exciting me all over again, but I wasn't about to tell him that. He'd think I was insatiable.

"I like that you're so sensitive to my touch." Roam rolled to his back, settling me on top of him without pulling out from inside me. "I need some time to recover, but let me show you a magic trick."

It was a weird time to start pulling rabbits out of hats or having me pick a card, but I was too in love to admit that.

Roam pinched my butt. "Not that kind of trick. I came up with this one after finding your vibrating worm drawer."

I didn't even blush. He had me far too curious about what he planned. The familiar heat of his magic warmed me where our bodies were joined.

Grabbing my hips, Roam lifted me, letting me see the thick raised ridges running down the front of his erection. Those ridges continued several inches, following the thin line of dark blue hair that ran up toward his stomach.

Roam's eyes glinted with devilish mischief as he lowered me, then rocked me forward and ground me down against him. The ridges provided friction in all the right places, and I nearly passed out at how incredible it felt.

My sexy djinn laughed. "I knew you'd enjoy this." He continued the steady rhythm, building my need to new heights.

I couldn't take it anymore and I begged, "Please, Roam."

"Tell me what you wish for." His hands gripping my hips kept me from taking matters into my own hands and finding my release.

His smile was teasing, but I saw the eagerness in his eyes. He was a djinn, and wishes were part of him. Just like writing your partner a love song, or baking their favorite dessert, this was an ability he wanted to use to make me smile.

Grinning in challenge, I purred, "I wish you'd stop teasing me and make me come so hard I lose my voice."

"With pleasure." He switched the pace so fast I barely had time to brace myself before I was seeing stars. "Now tell me who you belong to."

Once more I came apart, screaming his name until I couldn't speak at all.

"I will spend every day finding new ways to bring magic into your life." Roam rolled to his side, tucking my trembling body against his. "I love you, beautiful keeper of my heart."

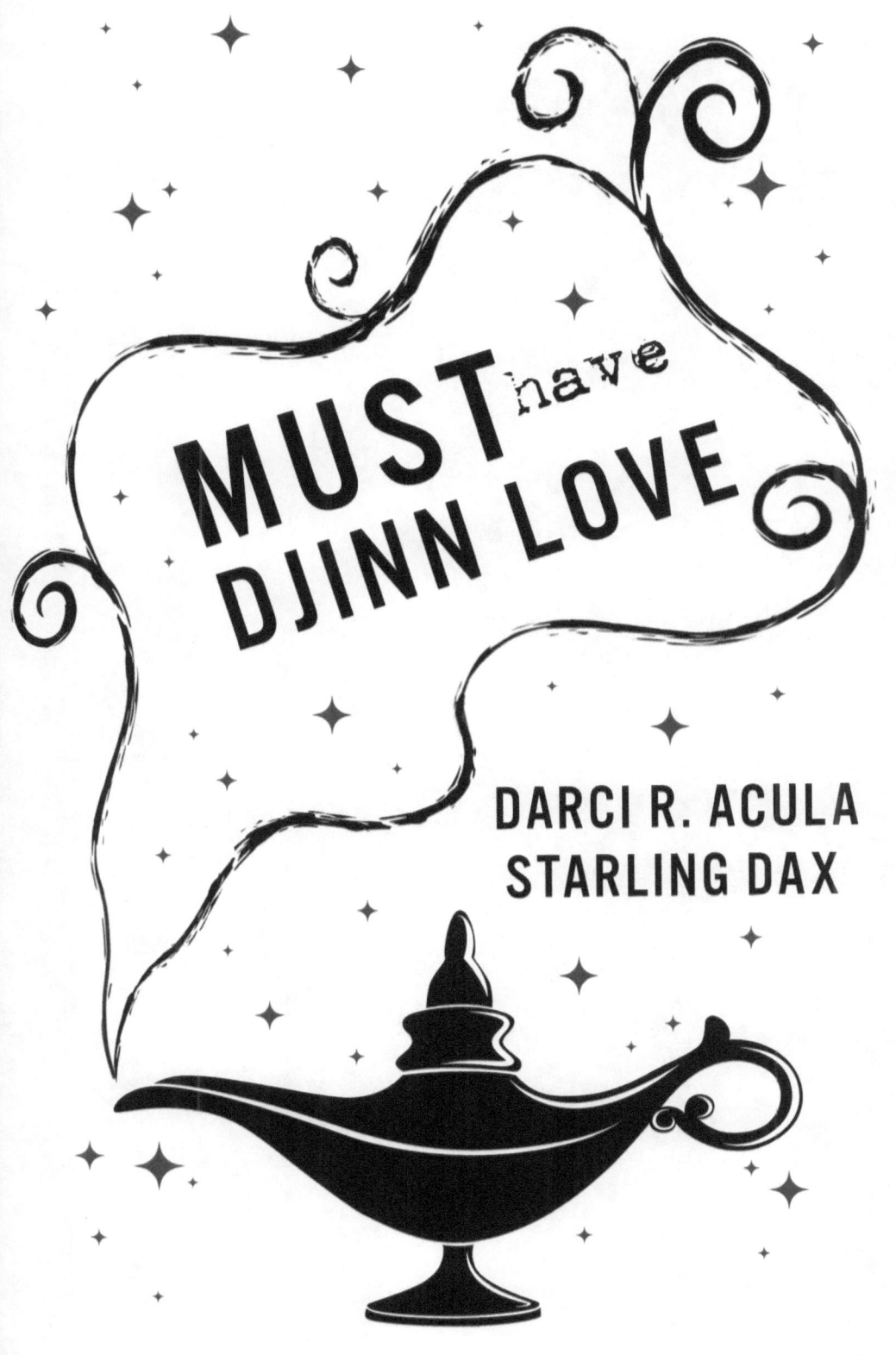

# MUST have DJINN LOVE

## DARCI R. ACULA
## STARLING DAX

CHAPTER I

jennie

"I wish I could meet a guy I have a connection with, or who isn't boring, at least."

"Sounds like you're used to bad dates," Camilla said, her fingers rotating the crystal figurine in her hands as she cataloged the item for auction.

I hadn't realized I'd said the words aloud until she spoke.

"No, they weren't bad, not really. Just…" I shook my head, not knowing how to explain it.

I'd never felt a connection or excitement. On every date I'd been on, it was as though my heart wasn't in it. But how do you tell someone that without sounding like a sociopath?

"I get it! Heaven knows I've had boring dates, too," Megan said, gently putting an antique book on the cart she was slowly filling. Her gloved hands protected the covers of the first-edition from the natural oils and moisture on her skin. "Don't go home with those guys; they have sex like someone who puts on a bib before eating. Zero out of ten stars."

A shocked laugh burst out of my chest, and I glanced over at Camilla, whose shoulders were shaking from giggles.

"I'm so glad I met you guys," she gasped.

It was something I was glad for, too. Because, in addition to meeting my two best friends, working at an auction house was a wonderful, hands-on way to learn as much as possible about the antiques I was interested in. I'd been working here for two years and had already learned so much.

Maybe the auction house wasn't meant to be my forever job, but at twenty-three, I didn't feel too pressed to figure out my future. And I loved it here.

The auction was scheduled for the next day because, according to my boss, the day before Valentine's Day was not a holiday. She'd ranted for the past week about how Valentine's Day was just a corporate scam designed to get more money out of hardworking people.

I disagreed. Although it wasn't like I had experienced anything other than the standard—a.k.a. boring—Valentine's clichés. Flowers. Chocolates. Cards filled with poetry.

They were empty gifts from men doing what countless ads told them they were supposed to do... all without putting in any real effort.

I blew out a sigh.

Maybe I had expected too much? I'd always tried to be romantic on my part and get something special for my partner as well. Perhaps I should've been grateful that at least a couple past boyfriends had tried to return the favor.

I'd certainly had other boyfriends with the same mindset as my boss—that Valentine's Day was nothing more than a cash grab by big corporations. Well, I still thought those guys had been tools, and I longed for some actual romance.

I wanted someone to romance me because they wanted to, not because they felt they had to. Someone I could share the excitement of being in love with.

"Do you have a date for Valentine's Day?" Camilla asked.

I wasn't sure if she was asking Megan or me or the room in general, so I didn't answer immediately. Picking up a heavy vase, I instead searched for the signature on the bottom to help guide me in determining its value.

"I do! He's hot, charming, and a business owner," Megan blurted, placing another first-edition book on her cart.

"Ooh, I love that for you," Camilla gushed.

"How about you two?" Megan asked.

Staying quiet, I moved on to another trinket—a little gold elephant statue that rested perfectly in the palm of my gloved hand.

"I'm going out with Tyler." Camilla had already told us about Tyler.

He was a trust fund guy with three degrees under his

belt and another he was currently working through. I didn't know where they found these guys, but I wished them all the happiness in the world.

"Jennie?" Megan prodded, and I glanced at her.

Her eyebrows were raised, and she studied me, waiting for my answer. Even Camilla watched me with keen interest as she picked up an oil lamp that looked brand new and old all at once.

I was momentarily sidetracked by the antique lamp and wondered if it had ever been used since it was rare to see such an old piece in near-perfect condition,

Shaking my head, I avoided their eyes. "No Valentine's date for me this year."

Not because I couldn't get one, but because none of the options were that appealing. I didn't say the last part out loud for fear of sounding like an awful human being. But I was tired of wasting time on the wrong guys. I wanted to find my Mr. Right.

"I should set you up with my cousin." Camilla drummed her fingers on the wooden table.

Um, was she crazy? Maybe she'd forgotten the stories she'd told us about her cousin.

"You mean the one who's currently playing the field and dating every girl who'll say yes at the same time? The same one who forgot his date's name four times during Thanksgiving?" Megan asked, voicing my inner thoughts.

"UGH! I still can't believe he actually brought a girl home to meet his parents." Camilla sounded mystified, and

I lifted both shoulders, glad the conversation had veered away from my love life.

"I bet she kept bringing it up, and he just brought her home to shut her up." Megan gave a terse laugh.

Camilla bobbed her head in agreement. "I bet you're right."

The conversation tapered off, and we continued cataloging the items up for auction. As we worked, I happened across something I'd never seen before and picked the object up with careful hands.

It was a beautiful jade container and instantly felt like a mystery to be solved. Turning it reverently in my hands, I analyzed it.

It was worn smooth, but the faint lines of a filigree pattern etched into the surface left me puzzled. The design work was unusual for the time period I was guessing the container had been created in. I'd never seen anything like the jade object, and I found myself driven to learn everything there was to know about it.

"Bye, Jennie! We're off to get waxed!" Camilla called in a sing-song voice, and I nodded, barely hearing her as I continued studying the object.

I tried to pull the top off, but it was stuck so tight, I gave up for fear of breaking the unusual artifact.

With the chatter of my workmates gone, I was left alone. The sudden silence of the room hit me like an arrow piercing my heart. My mind drifted from my work and back to the fact that everyone else had plans for Valentine's Day.

Maybe I should have just gone out with someone so I wouldn't be alone on the holiday, but I was tired of settling, and I wanted a real connection with the right man.

I sighed, hating that with each passing month, I was losing faith that I'd happen across the person for me. Tears burned the back of my eyes, but I refused to cry over my love life—or lack thereof.

Rubbing my thumb on the worn, smooth spot of the jade, I blinked back my tears. The filigree pattern seemed more heavily worn than the rest of the surface, and I wondered absently what had caused it.

"I wish I could have just one perfect Valentine's date," I mumbled under my breath.

CHAPTER 2

jovat the abominable

Y ou'd think after sleeping for years, I'd be better rested. Some days, I'd swear I wouldn't be able to summon the energy to drag myself out of my lamp.

But I had a job to do just like the rest of the world, so I *poofed* out, trying to rub the grit from my long nap out of my eyes.

"I can grant three wishes," I said, the words a crushing weight on my soul.

It was a lie my kind had perpetuated for as long as we had existed, and trust me, seeing the same kind of people day in and day out, century after century, had definitely tainted my view of people.

I mean, sure, they weren't all bad, but the ones I'd dealt with hadn't been shining examples of humanity.

"You what?" A young woman stared unblinking at me.

For a moment, I was speechless. I'd seen women over many centuries, but this one was by far the fairest.

Her heart-shaped face had a glow that came from being kissed by the sun and was framed by wild golden curls. Large dark eyes peered up at me, pulling on heartstrings I didn't think I possessed. There was a sweet openness in her expression rather than the greedy glint I was accustomed to.

I hadn't heard her wish, but I knew she was the one who'd awakened me, which meant she'd made a wish while rubbing my lamp.

"This can't be real." She slowly looked down at my home in her hands. "Besides, I thought your kind were in lamps?"

I crossed my arms. "What do you mean, *your kind?*"

She blushed, and a flash of embarrassment crossed her features. Intriguing.

Humans sure had changed a lot over the centuries. The last one I'd granted the wishes for had been a woman in long skirts. She'd worn so many layers, she looked like a bell. This one had on brown man pants, black boots that came up to her knees, and a black shirt that left her shoulders and arms bare.

"I kid, I kid." I chuckled, watching the fear drain out of her features. "We are typically found in lamps, but when one's home is broken, sometimes one has to improvise."

There wasn't much of a story to tell there.

Besides, I didn't mind the jade. It suited me and matched my eyes. I'd call that a win-win situation.

Turning slowly, I took in the room around us. The space

was a dusty little closet lined with shelves and filled with old garbage. How had I come to be here?

"So why were you in this?" Her eyes were shining with curiosity as she lifted my jade container.

Huh.

Nobody had ever asked me that before.

Most people jumped right into the wishing. *I wish, I wish, I wish.*

Blah, blah, blah.

But this one… she seemed more curious about *me* than what I would do for her.

"There's not much to tell." I waved away her question, but she seemed to be hanging on my every word. "Fine. An emperor, upset that he'd been granted his final wish, cast me out, cracking my lamp and forcing me to find a new home."

"What was the emperor's name?" she asked.

I lifted both shoulders. "Most people don't introduce themselves to me, and the ones that addressed him merely called him 'Emperor'."

A thought dawned on me. "You could wish for that information."

Her lips twitched. "Maybe I will. How long have you been slumbering?"

"What is the date?" I asked.

"2024."

I scratched my head. "My last owner used me in 1929. Something about getting revenge on her rich lover and his uppity family by disappearing their generational wealth."

Her eyes widened. "The stock market crash? That was you?"

I shook my head. "No, that was her wish. I merely granted her wish."

"That was devastating for a lot of families, not just that one family your owner wished it on." She sounded disappointed, and it bothered me.

Something in me wanted to smooth things over, to see her smile again.

"Contrary to popular belief, we can do anything. But some Djinn have their own code of ethics that prevents them from granting certain kinds of wishes, and they say that upfront. Riches are a common wish, although it was the first time I'd ever had someone wish for another person to lose their wealth. I didn't realize the devastation it would cause." I lifted both shoulders, well aware I couldn't atone for sins I'd taken part in in the past. "I do know I never want to anger a woman with a penchant for revenge."

She nodded her head as though agreeing with me.

"So, what wish can I grant for you today?" I repeated the question, wanting to get this handled swiftly.

The sooner I handled her wishes, the quicker I'd be able to get back to slumbering. I'd rather be sleeping than doing literally anything else.

"I don't want a wish." She looked up at me with those large brown eyes of hers.

"Come again?" I cupped a hand behind my ear, thinking maybe I'd misheard her.

Nobody had ever uttered those words in that order to me before.

"How come you don't talk all old-timey?" She tilted her to the side. "If you've been locked up for almost a century…"

I could practically see the wheels in her curious mind turning and found myself offering her the truth. "It's inherent. I don't actually speak your language, but we all have a curse—or blessing—that allows us to converse naturally with our lamp-holders. It helps to make sure there aren't any unfortunate mistakes during the wish granting." I bit the inside of my cheek to keep from laughing, then added, "And it isn't foolproof. Like that time when my last owner wished her ails away, and I thought she was talking about having a drinking problem… I'd made ale disappear and accidentally started the prohibition."

"That's horrible!" she exclaimed, but her lips twitched in amusement.

Her voice and expression both led me to believe she was truly interested in me, and it caused an odd heat in my chest. Was this the heartburn humans complained about?

"But enough about me. I can do anything you want except kill somebody." I smiled at her.

"Although, you could kill people if you wanted…" She arched a brow.

"Yes, I could, but please don't make me do that." I pinched the bridge of my nose.

"I was only teasing." She giggled. "I don't want to hurt anyone. Are you happy living in this?" She looked down at the jade piece in her hand. "I could find another vessel for you if this one isn't comfortable."

"I like my home," I replied, although I was touched by her question.

This human was unlike anyone I'd ever met, and I couldn't help but be curious about her.

"I don't exactly know how to tell you this, but you're going to be auctioned off to the highest bidder tomorrow." She worried her bottom lip between her teeth.

"Unacceptable. You woke me. I am yours until you exhaust your wishes."

The blonde shook her head. "I don't think my boss would find that an acceptable reason to allow me to keep you."

"So you must buy me." It was the obvious solution.

She let out a laugh. "Listen, I don't have that kind of money."

"You will." I crossed my arms over my chest.

The beautiful woman laughed harder, but I said nothing and simply basked in the glow of her joy.

Watching her wipe tears from her eyes, I found myself determined to make sure I stayed in her hands.

She didn't need to know I had lied. I could accept her refusal, return to my home, and go back to sleep until I was roused by my next owner, but I wanted to stay with this odd human and figure out how her strange mind worked. In a few short minutes, she was making me question everything I thought I knew about her kind.

And I was growing more curious about what she had wished for when she'd awakened me...

## CHAPTER 3

### jennie

I'd left his container at my work, but somehow, the Djinn had followed me home.

When smoke had poured from the jade, the last thing I'd expected was *him*.

How such a large, muscular man could fit in that tiny piece was beyond human understanding. His skin was periwinkle blue, his jade eyes glinted with mischief, and a dusting of turquoise freckles covered his nose and cheeks.

*He was freaking adorable!*

It had been hard not to take in the sheer size of his broad chest or to keep my eyes from drifting down the defined muscles to his tapered chest and lower...

When he'd first appeared, from the waist down, his body had been a cloud of glittering purple smoke, but on the walk home, he'd taken on a more human body. And although his body had legs, it was clear he didn't need them. More than once, I'd caught his feet floating a few inches above the pavement.

I wasn't sure if anyone else could see him, so I was glad we didn't run into anyone on the street.

For most of the night, I'd tried to get information out of him. After all, how often did you get a chance to learn about history through someone who was older than most of it?

Sadly, I hadn't gotten much out of him. The man had tighter lips than a grandmother who'd had an affair right around the time she'd conceived a child.

And I should know all about that since my grandma did it.

Covering my mouth, I tried to stifle my yawn. I'd stayed up too late, and now I was exhausted and trying to get ready to head for the auction.

"Are you sure this will work?" I asked.

"I'm sure." His unflappable confidence would've annoyed me if it had crossed the lips of any other man.

"Then let's do this." This was not how I envisioned spending the day before Valentine's Day, but I guess things could be worse.

The auction house was only a few blocks from my home —another reason I loved working there—so grabbing my leather backpack, I headed out the door.

My uninvited guest followed, phasing through the door. It was an ability I'd found unsettling last night until we set some ground rules. Number one on my list had been no intruding while I was in the shower—or while I was in the bathroom in general.

He'd scared the life out of me when I'd showered the night before by talking to me from the other side of the curtain. My scream had been worthy of an Oscar, but all I had to show for it was a sore throat.

I really should have been freaked out by the fact that a mythical being who shouldn't exist was following me around like a shadow. Why was I taking this so calmly?

Maybe he exuded something that naturally calmed the human who awakened him? Or maybe I just longed for any chance at excitement in my rather mundane life.

I locked the door and hurried toward my work. Along the way, the guy who lived at the end of my block, Dillon, waved from his mailbox as always.

"Working the day before Valentine's Day?" he asked, and I nervously glanced over at my companion.

"Don't worry, I'm invisible, and nobody can hear me," he assured me.

"Are you okay?" Dillon squinted at my face. "You look like you've seen a ghost."

I let out a nervous laugh, uncomfortable at how close he was to the truth. "I'm just stressed."

Dillion nodded. "I thought you didn't work on Tuesdays."

"Well, normally, I don't. But there's a big auction today, so…" I trailed off, letting him draw his own conclusions.

"Do you work tomorrow?" He leaned on the mailbox.

I shook my head.

"Hmm. I see. And do you have a date for Valentine's Day?" He arched an eyebrow at me, and I didn't like the direction the conversation had taken.

I tried to laugh him off. "I don't, but I made plans to date myself." It was a lie, but he didn't have to know that. "Self-love is the most important thing, right?"

Dillon opened his mouth, when a sudden sprinkling of rain fell around us.

"I better get going before I end up soaked." I thanked the universe for the small favor.

Dillon looked at the clouds, then gave a reluctant nod and headed toward his front door. Not waiting around, I hurried down the sidewalk toward work. Before we reached the auction house, the skies cleared up, and the rain dispersed.

"Thank goodness for that little sprinkle," I breathed.

"You appeared to be looking for a polite way out of that conversation," my companion stated.

My eyes widened. "That was you?"

He nodded, his sharp gaze studying my face.

I couldn't hold back a smile as I stopped, turning to face him and not caring if I looked like a crazy lady talking to herself in public. "Thank you. I've been wanting to ask… what's your name?"

He appeared taken aback, his brows shooting up his forehead. After a moment, his jaw relaxed, and he opened his mouth to speak but merely inhaled a breath.

It wasn't the first time he'd seemed surprised by something I'd said. The guy needed to get out more.

"Nobody has ever asked me that before," he murmured. "I'm Jovat."

"Just Jovat?" I asked, wondering why I'd expected some mystical name. Perhaps it was due to the countless mythology books I spent my evenings reading.

He rubbed a pale blue hand on the back of his neck, his lips curving up at the corners. "Well, my full name is Jovat the Abominable."

That was more like what I'd expected, but I didn't see anything about him that should have earned the title. "How'd you get that name?"

"I got wrapped up in a mess a few centuries ago. Nothing too big. It's a story for another time." His blue cheeks turned a pale purple. Was he blushing? "Besides, you probably already studied it in school."

"I like it. It's unique." I couldn't hold back a smile. "Well, Jovat the Abominable, let's get moving!"

Ten minutes later, I found an empty seat, watching people settle as the auction began. Jovat hovered just above the seat next to me, no doubt invisible to strangers. I had very little hope of winning him with the meager hundred dollars I had to my name, but I'd try because he asked me to.

Maybe he'd make other people not want him, and I would have an actual chance. Surely he possessed the power to do something like that?

I imagined there were some limits to what he could do

without me making an official wish, though. There was nothing to do but wait and see how things panned out.

In the meantime, I was living out one of my fantasies: collecting old artifacts I could treasure forever. I'd never been able to afford something like this, but the exercise was fun.

The bidding started on his jade home, and I lifted my hand. "Fifty!"

Heads turned, and my cheeks went red as the auctioneer scanned the room, refusing to even look at me.

"A thousand," someone said from the front row.

Well, that meant I was out.

"Will anyone give me two thousand?" the auctioneer shouted.

I sat there waiting for the next bidder to speak up and was stunned to feel my hand lift. Turning my head, I found Jovat's fingers wrapped around my arm, holding it up. What was he doing?

Opening my wallet, I angled it so he could see how empty it was. But instead, I found it was stuffed with more cash than it had ever held before. I caught the sparkle in Jovat's eyes.

He was putting the money in my wallet.

It was a smart move if he really wanted me to win this auction.

"Five thousand." Someone else raised their hand.

My heart pounded in my chest as I looked around the room. Jovat lifted my arm.

"Eight thousand." The words came from my lips, but I hadn't planned to say them.

Eight thousand was so much money.

"Ten."

"Twelve."

"Fifteen." As the people around me called out sums of money that made my head swirl, Jovat again lifted my arm.

"Twenty-five thousand." I snuck a sideways look at him.

Well, it seemed someone certainly knew their value and wasn't afraid to throw big numbers out there.

A tiny part of my heart warmed. Was he doing this to stay with me because he had to... or because he wanted to?

Jovat jerked his chin at my lap, and I could see my entire purse was bulging.

When the bidding finally closed for his jade home, I swear I went a bit cross-eyed handing over the huge stack of cash. I'd never imagined being able to buy my own collectible, but here I was, winning an auction for a piece I could only have dreamed about.

Once the auction ended, I moved to the back of the building and started helping Camilla and Megan pack the items in boxes to be sent out to the winners.

On our way back to my house, I pulled my phone out of my pocket. There was a missed call.

"I wish people would just text," I grumbled.

The phone instantly stopped ringing, and a text came through instead.

I jerked my head in Jovat's direction.

"I didn't mean to word it like that," I said, well aware I needed to watch what I said moving forward.

He gave me an innocent smile. "That wish was on me."

Why did that single sentence cause butterflies to flutter in my stomach? And why couldn't I stop wondering what his beautiful lips would taste like?

CHAPTER 4

Jovat
the abominable

"Tell me more about you." Jennie shifted on the couch, angling her body toward me.

I found I liked her attention being on me.

"There's not much to tell." I suddenly wished I had more of a story. "My whole life has revolved around granting wishes for others."

"Okay, but what about what you want?" she asked.

What did I want? Other than to slumber, I had never considered the question.

"I don't know what I want. It isn't something I've thought about." Wanting to keep her attention, however, I blurted, "I like slumbering between granting wishes for people."

"So… you like naps." Her lips curved up at the corners. "I do, too."

Her phone dinged, indicating a text had come through. "You better check that."

She shook her head. "I want to talk to you."

"But it might be something good."

Without taking her eyes off me, Jennie reached out and picked up her phone from the coffee table. Finally, she glanced down, and her expression drooped. "My boss is asking if I can put in a few hours tomorrow."

"I thought you loved your job?" I asked, confused by her reaction.

"Oh, I do." Her sad eyes and the downward curve of her lips contradicted her words.

Unsure what to do, I reached out and touched the top of her hand. With a hollow smile, she patted my hand on hers, still refusing to meet my gaze.

"How can I help?" I asked, suddenly hoping she wouldn't make a wish. Too bad I couldn't grant my own wishes.

"Some things can't be fixed," she said, finally meeting my gaze. "Wow. Your eyes are the same color as the jade you live in." Her breathy tone filled me with wonder, and I smiled.

My kind thought my home was ugly, but I'd loved it since I'd first set eyes on it. And now, a beautiful woman liked my place too.

"And your eyes are the color of the Sedona Mountains," I said, studying the rich red-brown hue.

"I swear I've heard the name Sedona before," she trailed off, and I sensed she was scouring every corner of her mind.

"Sedona is an incredibly beautiful city in Arizona." I hoped she'd conjured up the same rich brown bluffs and wavy cave walls I had.

"I don't travel much, but that must be where I've heard the name." She tapped at her phone and did a search. "Here we go! Wait, no. That's a person, not the city. Oh! There's the mountains."

Leaning her head and body toward me, she showed me the image, too. "The red rocks are so pretty," she breathed.

I wanted to tell her she was so pretty, but I held the words back. What if she thought I was patronizing her or just trying to make her feel better?

She was still focused on her phone's screen. "I never thought my eyes were all that pretty. They were just dirt brown to me." There was a longing note in her voice, and I wanted to pull her close and comfort her. "I love that you found something pretty where no one else has."

And with that, I gave in.

Wrapping my arms around her shoulders, I pulled her to my chest, wondering how she felt so small yet so significant. She leaned into me, lowering her phone and setting it beside her on the couch.

I liked this human with all her imperfections. Her goodness shone through, and I wondered why more people weren't like her. If they had been, maybe I wouldn't be so jaded about humanity in general.

Something clicked in my mind. Jennie was unique, one-of-a-kind, special. And for the first time in a thousand years—give or take a century or two—I wanted to be in a human's company longer than three wishes' worth of time.

"Are you going to tell me what is making you sad?" I prodded, wanting to find a way to cheer her up.

"I was sad… because I wanted to… Never mind. I knew it wasn't going to happen. But going into work makes it a reality." She stopped talking, abruptly closing her mouth as if she could swallow back the rest.

"What did you want?" I pressed.

"It's dumb." She sighed. "I want to have the perfect Valentine's date…"

Her words hit me like a right hook to the gut.

I didn't like the thought of her going on a date. Did she have someone in mind? Was it that strange man, Dillion?

As though reading my thoughts, she added in a voice barely more than a whisper, "With you."

Her teeth nibbled her lower lip, and I tried to sort through the flood of emotions rushing through me. She wanted a perfect date with me? I was the one she wanted?

Before I could fully absorb her words and understand them, she tilted her head back. Her gaze met mine, those beautiful eyes seeing me in a way no one before her had.

If I had a soul, she'd have been peering into it and ferreting out every secret I had… except *that* one.

Excitement slammed into my chest, stopping my heart for a second before the organ began beating double time.

Her gaze lowered to my mouth, and she leaned in, lightly pressing her lips to mine.

More than anything, I wanted to grant her heart's desire. But she hadn't made a wish.

# CHAPTER 5

## jennie

I'd texted my boss to tell her I couldn't work, so I'd been able to sleep in. But as I woke, staring up at my ceiling, something didn't seem right.

Turning my head on my pillow, I caught sight of Jovat as he stood beside my bed. He held a tray in his hands.

"What's this?" I rubbed my eyes, suddenly recognizing the smells—bacon, eggs, coffee...

"For you," he said as I sat up.

Jovat placed the tray on my bed, and I stared at him in confusion.

"You wanted the perfect Valentine's Day." His jade-colored eyes met mine.

"I didn't wish for it, though. And I said *date*, not *day*." I found I didn't mind the miscommunication.

"Jennie, I have free will. I can do things I choose to do." He reached out and gently stroked my cheek, his fingers warm and comforting. "And I choose to make your day special."

I teared up at the sweetness of his gesture and words. Nobody had ever wanted to make me feel special without some type of strings being attached.

"I've upset you. What did I say?" Jovat captured my face in both hands. Swiping his thumbs under my eyes, he brushed away the tears that had leaked from my eyes.

"It's happiness, I promise," I whispered, a little breathless at his unexpected touch.

"Happy tears?" He was skeptical, but when I nodded, his expression warmed.

With a quick motion, he leaned in and gave me a quick kiss. When he pulled away, my whole body cried out.

There was something so natural about the intimacy, and I found myself wishing for... well, more. Except I didn't make that wish out loud.

No, it was one of my inside wishes that I had no plan of letting out. The last thing I wanted was to make my three wishes and watch Jovat vanish out of my life.

Then again, I felt a bit bad about keeping him from his naps. I'd seen the love in his eyes when he spoke of sleeping, and I shared that love; just one more reason I was drawn to him. Part of me wanted to pull him onto my bed with me and spend all day in sleepy, cuddly bliss.

Though, I couldn't help but wonder if I had three wishes left now that he'd done this. I didn't want to ask because he was being so sweet. At least I knew I still had two wishes. That meant I could keep him with me for a while longer.

How could I let him go when the time came, though? I was drawn to him, and not just out of curiosity. It was more than that.

After breakfast, Jovat *poofed* a cushioned table into existence. "Time for a facial and full body massage." He rubbed his hands together. "Don't worry, I'm a licensed professional in both."

I couldn't hold back a laugh. "I haven't even gotten dressed yet!"

"Who needs to get dressed?" he asked. "This is your day, and you should be comfortable."

He had a point. I loved the idea of a pajama day.

With Jovat's guidance, I got on the table and laid down in my lady boxers and thin shirt. Part of me felt self-conscious about being nearly naked with him, but I was too intrigued by the idea of his hands on my body, so I quickly shoved those thoughts away.

I lay there while he wiped my face with a cloth. "What is your favorite comfort food?"

"This is kind of embarrassing, but ice cream and tacos." As I spoke, Jovat ran his hands over my face without actually making contact with my skin.

Delicious heat and steam emanated from his palms as he worked over every inch from hairline to collarbone. Jovat chuckled, moving in close as he worked, studying my face carefully.

"This part might tingle," he said, applying a mask to my skin.

As I lay there, I wondered how he knew what my

perfect date entailed.

"Is there anything else that could make your day perfect?" he asked, fanning my face with his hands.

The mask began to tingle. "I think you've nailed it."

He cleaned my face, gently applying a cooling cream that felt like heaven. "Roll over, Jennie."

I did as I was told, and he began to rub my body, starting at my shoulders and working his way down my back. Tension melted away from my body, and I moaned in delight.

He had magic hands. *Literally.*

Once I was reduced to little more than jelly, he had me roll over again and scooped me up. Cradled to his chest, I sighed in contentment as he carried me into the living room. The mouthwatering scent met my nose before I saw what was creating it.

Every surface, nook, and cranny held flowers of all types. There were so many I couldn't take them all in fast enough. My gaze landed on pastel purple lilacs, brilliant yellow sunflowers, richly hued lavender, royal plum-colored irises, pale pink lilies, and roses of every color imaginable.

Then I noticed the coffee table had been covered in different types of bouquets: fruit, chocolate, and cheeses, along with a bottle of wine chilling in an ice bucket.

"I can't believe you did this," I whispered as he set me carefully on the couch.

"Tacos and ice cream are on the menu, too." Jovat gave me a wink.

I wanted to ask if he was on the menu, but I was afraid it would scare him away.

"And," he added, revealing a stack of games. "We're going to have fun."

With that, he pulled Battleship out of the stack, and I sat forward.

"No way. This is war!" I said, opening the box and taking out my plastic grid.

As I settled into place, snacking on fruit and cheeses, I felt like the luckiest woman in the world. Jovat had perfectly nailed exactly what I had dreamed of in a perfect Valentine's date.

As we began calling out squares, I couldn't help but love that he'd planned the whole day around spending time together. It didn't matter what we did. The fact that we were focused on one another was exactly what I wanted.

Somehow, without even knowing what I wanted, Jovat had managed to create the day of my dreams.

No one else would ever top this. How could a regular man live up to what he had done for me?

I was in trouble.

There was no doubt in my mind that I was falling for Jovat.

I'd found my perfect man... *but he wasn't a man at all.*

# CHAPTER 6

## jovat the abominable

No human had treated me like a person before; I'd always just been a means to get what they wanted. A tool to be used, and then discarded with a look of disgust. Like a condom.

In return, I'd become indifferent when it came to humans. But when Jennie put her hand on mine, looked into my eyes, and spoke, my heart quivered.

"Thank you," she whispered.

The sweet curve of her lips and the way her eyes roamed my face made me smile. Other than her slip of the tongue, Jennie hadn't made a single wish.

Speaking of tongues, each time the tip of her pink tongue darted across her plump bottom lip, I longed to know what she tasted like.

But I desired more from her. I wanted…

What?

What did I want from this kind human woman?

To love her. To cherish her. To keep her safe when all hope seemed lost. To bring countless smiles to her lips. To share her joy and comfort her sorrows.

I wanted her in every way possible.

Well, maybe not in every single way—I didn't want to wear her skin or anything weird like that. I just want to love her freely and feel her love in return.

"No, thank you," I said, suddenly aware that I'd been staring at her without saying a word for far too long.

Her forehead creased and her confusion shone through in her voice. "What are you thanking me for? I didn't do anything."

We were sitting so close on the couch that our knees were almost touching. Her relaxed posture—elbow on the back of the couch, hand on her cheekbone supporting her head. With one leg tucked beneath her, her body spoke volumes about how comfortable and relaxed she was in that moment.

My stomach twisted uncomfortably. I was going to ruin that comfort.

"For being you," I said, reaching out to trace my fingertips along her cheekbone, in front of her ear, and along her jaw to her chin. She closed her eyes at my touch, then opened them, focusing on me.

"You goof. I'm not special." She let out a chuckle, popping a grape in her mouth from one of the fruit bouquets I'd covered the coffee table with.

I'd never met anyone like her, and that made her special to me. But how could I convey those thoughts?

With honesty. With a secret I'd kept guarded for as long as I'd been self-aware.

Looking into her eyes, I knew I had the power to destroy everything in this moment. Because I'd been lying to her from the start, and I wasn't sure if that'd change her mind about me.

"Something's bothering you," she said, her gaze tracing my face with concern.

"I want to tell you the truth." My heart thumped in my chest and I watched her expression change. But not to anger, just open curiosity.

"You don't owe me anything." She gave me a small smile.

"I told you I can grant you three wishes." The words tasted like ash in my mouth and I worried how she'd interpreted my words.

Jennie's lips turned down in a slight frown and her eyebrows lifted. "I don't care about that, Jovat." Her comforting tone turned something inside me to melted butter.

"I've never told anyone this, but I can grant as many wishes as I want." Speaking the truth felt incredible.

"I'm not interested in wishes, so it doesn't really matter to me if you can grant a thousand or none at all." Her hand found mine, squeezing gently. "I'm enjoying what's right in front of me."

I blinked hard. Perhaps being summoned by her was a

wish come true for me. No, that couldn't be. Djinn couldn't grant their own wishes.

Maybe all the time in solitude, never feeling seen, and always being disposable to people was clouding my judgment... but I suspected I was falling in love with her.

Jennie tilted her head, studying me. "I am curious, though. Why lie about it?"

I shrugged. "What better way to keep people from stringing me along their entire lives?"

"Ah, I see." Jennie tapped her finger on her chin. "That would really cut into your napping time."

"Exactly." Even though I recognized the gentle teasing in her words, I still worried she'd start to feel like she was inconveniencing me by keeping me from my beloved sleep.

But I knew that without hesitation, I'd choose her over slumber...

...if only she'd have me.

CHAPTER 7

jennie

If I was being one hundred percent honest, learning that Jovat could grant endless wishes was a bit of a blindside.

But I'd meant it when I said I didn't care. I didn't want wishes.

I wanted Jovat, because he was thoughtful, attentive, intelligent, and, well, *adorable*. Biting my lip, I tried to hide my smile, but nothing escaped Jovat's sharp jade eyes.

"And what do you find so amusing?" His fingers slid across my cheek.

I wanted to throw my arms around his neck and squeeze until he begged me to stop. Restraining myself, barely, I admitted, "I was thinking your name should be Jovat The Adorable, not Jovat The Abominable."

The faint lines around his eyes softened. "You've given me a name?"

I was unsure how to respond, and hoped I hadn't offended him with my teasing. "I'm not saying you have to change your name! I just think it fits a little better."

"Then Jovat The Adorable it shall be." He locked gazes with me. "It is an honor to receive a name from you."

His freckles began to sparkle like stars against his beautiful blue skin. It was both mesmerizing and alluring, and I found myself attracted to him in a way I'd never been attracted to another.

And while I couldn't help but wonder what other secrets he'd been keeping, I also wondered if I should care. He had all the right in the world to have and keep his secrets.

Plus, judging by the way I was growing more desperate for his touch, it was too late to protect myself. I was already falling for him.

Before I could speak, Jovat leaned in.

The magic man had to have been reading my mind, because how else could he so perfectly know exactly what I wanted and needed?

Every minute of my Valentine's Day had been utterly perfect, right down to the conversation, and now, a kiss.

His lips met mine, causing my heart to flip-flop wildly behind my ribs. He was soft and gentle. The kiss was innocent. But that wasn't what I craved.

Finding his large hand, I laid it on my thigh. Then, lacing my fingers around the back of his head, I opened my mouth for him.

Our tongues met, and his hand slid up my leg, leaving

my skin heated with excitement. There was nothing I wanted more than for Jovat to move his fingers higher, touching and exploring every inch of me.

His tongue teased mine, swirling around as his sweet flavor hit my system like a shot of whiskey. I moaned, and he swallowed the sound with a hungry groan of his own.

Jovat's body moved closer to me, running his hand up my hip and behind my back. His powerful arm gripped me, closing the gap between our bodies and holding me tight against him as we both rose to our knees on the couch.

His arms felt like coming home.

He broke the kiss, his breath cool against my damp lips as he spoke. "Are you sure this is a good idea?"

"Nope," I answered him honestly.

The thing was, I didn't care. I wanted this spark, this excitement, this runaway desire warming my insides.

"Do you want this?" I asked.

In response, Jovat sat down on the couch and pulled me onto his lap. He turned me so that I faced away from him, my back pressed to his chest.

Shifting his hips slightly, he rubbed himself against me, quickly removing all doubt about whether he wanted me as much as I wanted him.

"I really want to make a rubbing the lamp joke right now," I murmured, absolutely breathless.

"I dare you." His eyes crinkled at the corners in amusement and he planted a kiss on my cheek. Then his eyes darkened, and when he spoke, his voice had turned to a deep rasp. "Actually, since you've already rubbed mine, maybe I should return the favor and rub yours?"

A shiver raced through me as his hand slid down my hip, then under the waistband of my thin, fitted boxers. When his fingertips found the slick proof of my excitement, I sucked in a harsh breath.

All thoughts deserted me as he discovered my sensitive bundle of nerves and stroked. I couldn't focus on anything with his fingers moving back and forth, then in an expert dance that had darkness blurring the edges of my vision.

"You really do have magic hands," I breathed, my voice trembling.

I guess he needed to prove his lips were magic too, because he began kissing and sucking his way down my neck and across my shoulder. Each time I shifted my hips in response to his touch, I'd feel an answering jerk from his erection beneath me.

He was driving me crazy, and it was becoming impossible to keep from writhing on his lap. I could feel pleasure threatening to explode, but I fought against the tidal wave. How was it possible for him to affect me so quickly with just his touch?

"Jovat. I'm... I'm going to..." I whimpered, and he stared down at me.

Heat and hunger clashed in his incredible eyes, and his fingers began to stroke me harder, driving me toward my inevitable release. My legs began to flex and my stomach knotted up, but still I tried to fight the impending release welling up in me.

"Your body is so responsive to my touch." His husky purr vibrated through my body. Bringing his lips to my ear, he whispered, "It's almost like you're mine."

All thoughts blinked out of existence and the blood thundering in my ears drowned out every other sound. A gasp wrung from my lips as blinding pleasure exploded through my body, sending ripples of heat dancing along every nerve ending.

Jovat continued to move his fingers, but far slower and gentler. He held me to him, as my body jerked and trembled, whispering as his lips kissed my neck, cheek, and temple.

I had no idea what he was saying, but the warm tone and cadence relaxed my body. No one had ever made me feel like he had, and as I melted into him, he snuggled me close.

A thought popped into my mind and the words tumbled from my mouth before my brain could vet the comment. "How old are you?"

"About a thousand years, give or take a few centuries."

"Give or take a few *centuries*?" That was a huge margin!

"When you live as long as my kind, you lose track. I'm young for a Djinn."

That made me pause, not quite sure how to feel about his words. "Well, talk about an age gap relationship."

He chuckled. "In terms of my kind, I'm about the same age as you."

"Thanks—wait! Are you calling me old?"

He laughed, threading his fingers with mine as we sat on my couch.

In the quiet of the room, cuddled in his arms, I realized what I wanted to do for him. He'd been so amazing, made me feel things, given me the perfect Valentine's Day... something I'd been worried I'd never find.

My heart constricted as I thought about my plan.

I wanted to free him.

Nobody should live their lives trapped in service of others.

"Can I... free you somehow?" I whispered. "Would you want to be free?"

He went still, and I snuck a peek up at him. Jovat seemed stunned, unsure how to respond to me.

Finally, he cleared his throat. "Why would you want to do that?"

"Because no one should have an unhappy life serving others. But if you're happy and I'm wrong about the situation, I apologize." I couldn't breathe as his eyes narrowed, studying me.

As the silence stretched on, the finality of what I'd said sank in and I realized what wishing him free would mean. Letting Jovat go.

He might have decided to walk right out of my life forever.

But I needed to do the right thing for him.

Jovat deserved the world, and I wanted to help him get started.

# CHAPTER 8

*jovat the abominable*

Jennie had no idea what she was offering me. Scooping her up, I carried her toward her bedroom, all the while wondering how to navigate her request.

She couldn't wish me free, not exactly.

"You didn't answer." Her arms looped around my shoulders as I carried her. "And I can walk."

"I like carrying you." My arms tightened around her small body. "Are you still hungry?" I asked, wanting to be sure she went to bed one hundred percent happy, satisfied, and as well taken care of as possible.

She nodded her head as I lowered her onto the edge of her bed.

"What would you like to eat?" I asked, my heart still tugging as I thought about her wanting to free me. Not only had no one ever treated me like a living, breathing being, no one had ever given a thought to me, my life, my wants, or my desires.

I was a tool to be used, nothing more. So when Jennie had told me she wasn't special... I couldn't have disagreed more.

"I'll get you anything you want," I prodded, wondering why she was hesitating.

She tried to speak, but sounded almost as if something was caught in her throat. Was she regretting her choice to try and free me?

"I didn't hear you," I said, kneeling before her and peering up into her eyes.

The tears welling there had me reaching for her face and wanting to comfort her. "Fettugenie."

I stared at her in shock for a second as a smile spread across her face.

"Get it? Fettu-*genie*?" A laugh broke from her lips and she fell back onto the bed, literally rolling with laughter at her terrible pun.

She was adorable, incorrigible, and the kind of woman I could imagine spending my next thousand years with. My lips twitched as I schooled my face into a playful scowl. She giggled until tears streamed down her cheeks.

Chuckling under my breath, I shook my head and willed her request into existence. A table set for two, wine, and fettuccine appeared beside the bed.

The joy in her face as she took in my work lit me up from inside, making me feel light on my feet.

"Is wine okay?" I asked, glancing over to see her

pushing herself into a sitting position, a wide smile on her face.

She nodded. "I'd rather have a... have a..."

I recognized the telltale scrunching of her nose that preceded her little jokes, and I patiently waited to see what she came up with this time.

"A Djinn and tonic." Unable to keep a straight face, she dissolved into laughter.

I couldn't help joining in her little game. "I think you'd better have a Djinn-ger ale instead."

The room went silent.

I froze.

She froze.

We stared at one another for a moment.

Then we burst into loud, wheezing laughter. Had I ever laughed this hard? I didn't have to think hard about the answer. No one had ever brought this much joy into my life.

"Okay, come sit down." I pulled out her chair for her.

With her shoulders still shaking, Jennie slipped off the bed and sat down. I scooted her chair in. Even though I knew it went against her desire to stay home all day, I willed us to a new location.

Jennie let out a little yelp, gazing around. Her knuckles turned white as she gripped the seat of her chair with both hands.

Wanting to calm her fears, I reassured her. "You're safe. No one can see us. And you can't fall."

Looking down, she studied the surface of the calm lake that was about fifty feet below us. Her stunning face was illuminated by the soft reflected glow of the stars and the candles dancing in the air around us. Off in the distance, mountains reached for the sky, their peaks white with snow. Her gaze finally drifted back to me after taking in her surroundings.

"This is beautiful." She breathed the words, and I internally sighed with relief.

And I was done holding back. I wanted to win her heart. "You are beautiful."

I took the chair opposite her and sat down. The darkness around us—lit only by stars—offered just enough glow to see one another as she smiled.

"It's the shadows playing tricks on your eyes." She picked up her wine glass.

"I can't be fooled, love." The second I said the words, she went still, watching me.

I'd called her love. If she'd had any doubt about my feelings for her, she wouldn't now. Swallowing back my nerves, I picked up my wineglass and lifted it toward her.

Jennie blinked, then touched the rim of hers to mine with a delicate *tink* before taking a sip, her gaze never leaving my face.

"So, how do I free you?" she asked, picking up her fork and swirling noodles around the tines.

After I'd granted three wishes for my previous owners and they'd believed I was useless to them, they'd tossed away my home as though it had been trash. But Jennie had witnessed my power, and she still wanted to free me.

Why didn't she want to keep me captive? Why didn't she want to beg me to do this for the rest of her life?

Who would pass up the opportunity to be spoiled like this every day for the rest of their lives? I'd told her the truth—that I could do this forever.

Unless she freed me.

I sipped the fruity wine. I had no need to eat, but over the centuries, I'd learned people found someone sitting with them at a meal and not eating rather unsettling. Now that habit gave me a chance to pause, reflect, and try to figure out what to say and do next.

"It can't be done," I said.

Her smile fell away, and her eyes shimmered with tears. "You're trapped forever with no way to escape?" The waver in her voice sliced me to the bone and nicked my heart.

I needed to be honest. "It's a question that has been asked since the dawn of Djinn. The answer is that we cannot be freed, but we can be wished human."

"I wish—"

I lifted a hand, cutting her off before she could say the words. "But I'll be human. Not a Djinn. I'll grow old like a human, I'll eventually die like a human, and I'll never be able to grant another wish as long as I live."

The gravity of my statement seemed to strike her like a physical blow; she sat back in her chair, watching me as I waited for her response.

"Is that what you want? To be human? Or, if you had the choice, would you stay a Djinn forever?" Her eyes searched my face as a slight wind we couldn't feel because of the protective barrier I'd put around us stirred the waters below us.

What did I want? I searched my mind, but the only answer I could dig up was that I wanted *her*.

But would she want me if I no longer had magic? When I could no longer will her desires into existence, would she still be interested in me?

"I… would want to be free." The honest words left my lips, and she nodded. "But wait until we're back home, because I don't want to go for a swim and have to figure out how to get us back."

Jennie laughed, then reached out and put her hand on mine. "Agreed. Let's enjoy this delicious meal. When we're home, I'll wish you free."

As she spoke, pain flashed across her face and I wondered what caused it.

"Are you okay?" I interlaced our fingers.

Her expression cleared, and a smile curved up the corners of her lips. "Yes! I'm excited. Now, tell me more about what you're going to do when you're human."

"Well, I think I'd like to find love, settle down, maybe think about having a family." I shrugged, trying to appear relaxed.

In truth, my heart was thumping at the possibility of being free. Warmth flooded through every vein, along every nerve end, from the top of my head to the tips of my fingers, to the bottom of my feet and into my toes.

I'd never dreamed this could happen for me.

"Settle down, Romeo," she teased, taking a bite of her

food. Despite her humor, there was a sad note in her voice that I was struggling to decode.

"I'm sure you're going to find someone who deserves you and loves you more than anything." Her fingers squeezed mine, then she pulled away.

That thought hurt. I wanted her to be the one I enjoyed life beside. But maybe I'd read her all wrong.

As we finished out our meal, she rubbed her hands down her thighs, watching me with an open expression. "I think it's time."

With a nod, I willed us back to her home.

"Are you ready, Jovat The Adorable?" she asked.

I took a moment to gather myself, then blew out a long sigh. "Yes."

She took my hands in hers as we stood face to face. "I wish you free, whole, and happy, and for all your dreams to come true as a human."

I hesitated.

"Did it work?" she asked.

I shook my head. "You might want to remove the part where all my dreams come true."

If all my dreams came true, she might find herself in an uncomfortable situation. My magic was powerful and I could absolutely make people fall in love.

I wanted Jennie, but I didn't want her to love me for my magical abilities... or because the magic made her believe she loved me back.

## CHAPTER 9

### jennie

My brow creased at his odd request. Once he was human, he could live his life however he wanted. So why was he asking me to reword my wish?

But as I stared into his eyes, I couldn't quite muster up the courage to ask why. We only had moments left together, because once this wish was granted, I knew he'd move on. He'd live his life the way he'd planned, and I'd be nothing more than a memory.

Setting him free meant losing him… which hurt more than anything. But I didn't want to burden him with my heartache.

Jovat deserved to live life his way, on his terms, and with whomever he fell in love with. He should get to do things the way he wished. I would have laughed at my pun, but I was finding it too hard not to cry.

My heart longed to keep him, not as a wish-granting-Djinn, but as mine to love.

Straightening my spine, I shoved aside my selfish desires. I could sacrifice my happiness for his.

"I wish you free, whole, and happy, as a human." I held my breath, but again, nothing happened. "Did it work?"

"I'm... not sure." He didn't seem to know, and my heart spasmed.

It was hard enough doing this knowing I would lose him, but knowing I'd have to repeat it yet again was a special kind of torture.

But before I could speak, three men materialized in my room. A sense of dread welled up in me as he shifted me behind him, as if protecting me.

"Jovat The—"

Jovat cut in, "Jovat The Adorable."

Two of the men ran their hands over their lips, and it took a moment for the first guy to speak again. "Jovat The Adorable, this person has wished you human."

Jovat tilted his head in acknowledgement, while still keeping me behind him.

"Is this acceptable to you?" the one in the middle asked. "Giving up your magic to become a mortal man who will grow old and die on their timeline?"

The Djinn speaking almost reminded me of Santa, with his close-clipped white beard and thick white hair that hung to his shoulders. But he was built like a lumberjack, which really would have confused my whole being if I wasn't already head over heels for Jovat.

Lowering his head, the first Djinn shook his head in seeming disbelief. When he lifted his head to stare directly at me with bright blue eyes, I wanted to duck behind Jovat again. His sharp gaze seemed almost... accusatory, like he believed I'd talked Jovat into this against his better judgment.

The third one hadn't said a word. He merely stood, watching us with russet brown eyes.

"Yes." Jovat's voice held an edge, and I peeked around him again.

Were they about to start a war? Jovat had told me he was young by Djinn standards, but he was incredibly powerful.

If four Djinns started fighting, I doubted it was going to go well for humans. I'd never even thought to add *Djinn meeting in my bedroom* to my apocalypse bingo. Sheesh, that sounded wrong.

"Then human you become." As the first Djinn said the words, buff Santa stepped forward and Jovat lifted his hands at his sides, staring down at them. Was it working? Could he feel the magic draining from his body?

The three stood, watching and waiting for something.

"Thank you." Jovat bowed to the three before turning to face me.

A bittersweet feeling rose in my chest as his jade green eyes met mine. I wanted him to know how much I liked him—no, how hard I was falling for him. But there was no way I could say the words around the lump in my throat.

He'd truly made my life magical and perfect in the short time I'd known him.

"Can I make one last wish?" I whispered.

Sadness flickered in his eyes as he spoke. "I don't have magic anymore, Jennie."

"I think you can help me with this one."

"Sure, anything for you," he said with a nod of his head.

"Can you make sure I don't die a virgin?"

He lifted an eyebrow at me, a mischievous smile on his lips. "I just said I don't have magic. I can't make you immortal."

I let out a shocked gasp and slapped him playfully on the shoulder. "I wish you knew how much I love you."

I froze.

He froze.

Had I really just said those words?

Jovat swallowed. "I think I can."

"What?" I didn't understand.

"Wish for something else. Something tangible, quick," he said, his words commanding and sharp.

Faced with a mixture of his excitement and my own panic, my mind blanked and I blurted out, "I wish I could Djinn and bear it!"

He stopped, his expression shifting into the disappointed dad look he did so well.

I lifted both hands and shoulders. "I can't help it!"

"If everyone knew that becoming human with magic was an option, our kind might have died out a long time ago." At the unfamiliar voice breaking into our private moment, I jolted in shock.

I'd forgotten about the three Djinn in my room. How embarrassing.

Jovat turned to face buff Santa as if waiting for more of an explanation. But they had nothing further to say and faded away.

"Are they gone this time?" I asked, peeking around him.

He nodded.

"So, you still have magic?" I asked.

He continued nodding, looking down at his hands.

"And how does that make you feel?"

"Happy, because it means I can spoil you the way you deserve." He turned to me once more, taking my face in both his hands and kissing me.

Stunned, I pulled away. "Are you saying you want *me*?"

He had magic.

He had freedom.

He could do anything he wanted.

"You know you could make a supermodel or movie star fall in love with you. I mean, that chick from—"

Jovat kissed me again.

And again, I pulled back. "You can't silence me with kisses!"

"I don't want to silence you, but I really want to kiss you," he grumbled, kissing me again.

"Besides"—Jovat's lips brushed mine as he spoke—"I'm pretty sure you had another wish for me."

My cheeks blazed red hot, and I regretted bringing it up.

"You can tell me what the perfect first would be for you, or I can decide." He spoke the words in his deep, throaty voice, and my heart began to pound.

I wanted him.

I longed for him more than I'd ever wanted anything or anyone in my life.

Thinking back over the day, and how perfectly amazing dinner over the lake had been, I grinned. Never, in a million years, would I have dreamed up something so romantic, fun, and thrilling.

"I think I'll let you decide," I said, trusting him in that moment with everything I was, everything I wanted, and everything we could be.

As I wound my arms around his neck, I had one more thing to say. Well, one more thing to say before he whisked me away.

I stared into his eyes. "You granted the wish I didn't ask you for, as if you somehow knew what my heart wanted all along."

Flattening my palm to his chest, I felt the steady thump of his heartbeat against my hand. When I looked up into his face again, his jaw flexed as if struggling to find the words he wanted to say.

"And you granted my wish by wanting to spend time with me." His words and the sweet look in his eyes melted me like a chocolate bomb in hot milk.

On an unrelated note, I had a sudden craving for hot cocoa.

"I love you, Jennie," he whispered.

Warmth blossomed in my chest, and I responded. "And I love you, Jovat The Adorable."

# ABOUT DARCI R. ACULA

Darci R. Acula is Sedona Ashe's not-so-secret pen name. Sedona's books tend to focus on Reverse Harem relationships, while Darci's books feature only MF relationships.

Darci (aka Sedona) doesn't reserve her sarcasm for her books; her poor husband can tell you that her wit, humor, and snarky attitude are just part of her daily life. While she loves writing paranormal shifter reverse harem novels, she's a sucker for true love, twisted situations, and wacky humor.

Darci lives in a small town at the base of the Great Smoky Mountains in Tennessee. She and her husband share their home with their three children, adorable pup, five cats, pet arctic fox, chickens, several crazy turkeys, two chubby frogs, and over a hundred other reptiles. When she isn't working, she enjoys getting away from the computer to hike, free dive, travel, study languages, and capture images of places and animals through her photography. Darci has a crazy goal of writing a million words in a year, and spending six months exploring Indonesia.

www.darciracula.com